Mr. Darcy: The Key to Her Heart

By Zoe Burton

Mr. Darcy: The Key to Her Heart

Zoe Burton

Published by Zoe Burton

ISBN-13: 978-1-953138-19-4

Acknowledgements

First, I thank Jesus Christ for being my Savior, my Rock, and my Guide. I cannot do this without You. I love you!

As always, I thank Rose and Leenie for their friendship and their feedback. I love you, too. <3

Finally, thanks go to my wonderful Patreon patrons, whose support lets me know that what I write is important to them, and to the world.

Chapter 1

Netherfield Park, Hertfordshire

July 22, 1805

Fitzwilliam Darcy felt his father's travelling coach slow down and closed his book. Tucking the small volume into his pocket, he turned his head toward the window to see that the equipage was approaching a large, stately, red-brick house. He pulled on his gloves and donned his hat, then picked up his walking stick and rested it across his knees. His mind wandering, he wondered why such an accessory had become fashionable for the young and able-bodied. The carriage stopped, drawing his attention back to the events at hand. When the door opened, he stepped out.

"Welcome to Netherfield, Cousin!" Andrew Darcy hastened from the house. At twenty, he was two years younger than his visiting relative and still a student at Cambridge.

Fitzwilliam Darcy grinned. "Thank you. I am happy to be here." He looked up at the five-story dwelling. "This is a very pretty house. It is nothing to Pemberley, of course."

Andrew laughed and clapped his cousin on the shoulder. "Nothing compares to Pemberley, I know, but it *is* a very fine building, and my mother has made it a pleasant place in which to reside, despite the neighbors." He gestured toward the door. "Come in. Mother and Father are eager to see you."

Darcy wondered what his cousin had meant by his comment about the nearby residents. He had no time to inquire at the moment, so he tucked it away into the back of his mind for investigation at a later date. He followed Andrew into the house and up a wide staircase to the first floor, then down the hall and into a beautifully-decorated drawing room.

Andrew announced Darcy's arrival to his gathered family. "He is here!"

"So I see." An older gentleman who shared Darcy's coloring stood, as did three females and a boy who were nearby. "You would have done better to allow the housekeeper to perform her office."

Andrew shrugged. "It was just as easy to do it myself."

The elder gentleman stepped toward Darcy. He bowed, then reached for the younger man's hand to shake it. "Welcome to Netherfield!"

Darcy bowed. "It is good to see you, Uncle Joseph."

"I was delighted when your father told me to expect you to attend our house party." Joseph gestured toward the rest of the family. "Your aunt and cousins await you."

Darcy nodded and took the three steps from where he had been standing to where his aunt stood. "It is good to see you, as well, Aunt Theodosia." He bowed.

"It has been too long. Look at you! You have grown into such a tall, well-formed young man. Your mother would be proud."

Darcy blushed. "Yes, ma'am."

"Grace, Augusta, come greet your cousin."

The young ladies stepped forward and curtseyed. Grace, a tall, fair, willowy blonde of seven and ten years, greeted him first. "I am pleased you could come. You missed my coming out ball, you know. If not for you, who I am already acquainted with, this house party would be ever so boring."

"I am at your service." Darcy bowed to her again. "What shall be my task, fighting off eager suitors or pushing them towards you?" His lips twitched, though he strove to keep his features set into a smooth mask.

Grace giggled. "Neither. I am not ready to marry, but I do like to flirt. You may simply be a friend and tell stories of our adventures as children when called upon."

Darcy heard Andrew snort from somewhere to his left. He remained as sober of countenance as he could manage, though, as he replied. "Your wish is my command." A movement from his next youngest cousin drew his attention.

"I am happy you are here, as well. You can help me convince Mama that I should be out already, for I long to attend the amusements that are planned, and there is no law that says I must remain in the schoolroom until Grace marries." Augusta Darcy was the opposite of her sister, short, petite, and dark, with long curls hanging down her back.

"I do not know that I am the best one to help you with that task." Darcy shook his head as he spoke. "Do not be in such a hurry to grow up. Enjoy your childhood while you can."

"If I have told you once, Augusta, I have told you a dozen times, I do not care what that Bennet hoyden is allowed to do, you will not be out at fifteen." Theodosia's hands landed on her hips. "Not another word about it or you will be banished to the nursery for the duration of the party. Do you understand me?"

With a roll of her eyes and a huff, Augusta grudgingly agreed. "Very well, but when I perish from boredom, you will cry bitter tears over your lack of care." She crossed her arms and dropped into a chair.

Not knowing what to say to such dramatics, Darcy chose instead to turn to his right, where a gangly boy who was the image of his father stood. "Frederick, how are you?"

The boy bowed. "I am well, thank you." He blushed when his voice cracked. Clearing his throat, he continued. "Andrew tells me you have completed your University courses and will be going on a Grand Tour in the spring."

"I have, and I will. I look forward to seeing all the places I have learned about."

Frederick grinned. "I would love to travel to exotic places. Not just the Continent, but the Indies and the Orient, as well." His face fell. "But, I do not know how it will happen, as I must choose a trade."

"Perhaps the army or the church would allow you to travel. One of my Fitzwilliam cousins is in the regulars. I will write to him and find out for you, if you like, at least about the army."

Frederick's face lit up again. "You would do that?" When Darcy nodded, the boy continued. "Thank you! Please do write to him. I will pay the postage out of my allowance."

Darcy chuckled. "That will not be necessary, but I will write to him immediately."

Theodosia smiled fondly at her youngest son. "There, now your mind will be at ease, at least for a while. I suggest, however, that you speak to the rector about the church before you make your final decision. You do have time, you know. You must finish at Eton and then attend University before you do anything."

"Yes, ma'am." Frederick's grin did not dim, but he did sit down beside his elder brother.

Theodosia turned back to her nephew. "Now that you have greeted everyone, I am sure you would like to wash the dust of the road away. I will have Mrs. Nichols show you to your room. We have kept town hours, for the most part, so we will not eat until much later. However, we will serve tea and a light meal in an hour. We expect more guests to arrive this afternoon."

Darcy's brows shot up. "Am I the first?"

"You are." Theodosia's eyes twinkled. "I attribute that to your Darcy need for promptness."

Darcy blushed. "You are undoubtedly correct. I do hate to be late."

His aunt patted his arm. "Do not be embarrassed. Your uncle and at least one of your cousins is the same way. We are used to such things in this household." Theodosia paused and tipped her head toward the door. "There is the housekeeper. Follow her, and hurry back so we can eat."

Darcy bowed and did as instructed.

When he arrived at his room, he discovered that his valet, Mr. Smith, had already laid out fresh clothes and had ordered up a bath.

"It was a rather dusty ride, and I assumed you would wish to be clean sooner rather than later."

Darcy nodded. "You are correct, I would wish it so. We have an hour to get me clean and dressed and back in the drawing room."

With a tip of his head, Smith retreated to the dressing room, and Darcy soon heard water being poured into a tub. He wandered about the room as he tugged at his cravat. It was a comfortable chamber, with a masculine feel to the decoration. The bed was large, which was a relief. He was a tall man, and well-formed, with wide shoulders. Small beds were often uncomfortable for one of his size. He stepped across to the windows that lined the wall opposite the bed. The view was spectacular. This room overlooked the gardens, which included a large area of roses, a maze, and, off in the distance, a folly.

With a grin, Darcy turned from the window, tugging his tailcoat off as he went. He could not remove it himself, as it was tightly tailored, but by the time he reached the dressing room door, Smith had appeared again and assisted in its removal.

Soon, Darcy was in his bath and lost in thought about his relatives. He did not often see this branch of his father's family. The Darcys were known to have small numbers of children, or at least few who survived to adulthood, and of those, most were girls, who could not inherit. Darcy and Andrew shared a great-grandfather, which, if he understood correctly, made them second cousins. They were not so far apart that they could claim a great distance between the branches, but not so close that they ran in the same circles, either.

Joseph was a judge, and a very successful one. Darcy's father, George, corresponded with his brother on a regular basis, and the families gathered once or twice a year to visit. Darcy himself did not always attend the gatherings once he began at Cambridge, but he knew his cousins relatively well.

Darcy remembered Andrew's comment about the neighbors and experienced a pang. *I must ask him what he meant by that,* he thought. *I should like to know if there is something untoward about them.* His aunt's remark about some Bennet female being a hoyden passed through his mind next, and he decided he ought to ask about that, as well.

His bath complete, Darcy allowed his man to assist him in dressing, standing very still while Smith tied a fashionable knot in his cravat. His stomach rumbled and he rolled his eyes when his long-time servant tried to hide a smirk.

"There. It is as perfect as I can make it." Smith stepped back and examined his work with a critical eye. "Yes; I can do no better." He bowed. "Enjoy your meal, sir."

"I intend to." Darcy paused. "I do not know why I am asking this of you, but please keep an ear out belowstairs for gossip. What we should know about the neighbors and all that." Darcy waved his hand around to the right, as though to encompass the room.

"I will do that." Smith bowed again and retreated.

Darcy arrived at the drawing room to find his aunt alone.

"There you are." Theodosia rose gracefully from her seat near the window. "Let me call for tea and the rest of the family. They have all scattered, I fear. None of them are much good at waiting." She laughed, the tinkling sound making her nephew chuckle along.

Darcy stood, waiting for his aunt. When she finished with the housekeeper, she walked toward him and gestured to the seating area. "Sit down here with me. Tell me about your father and sister. How are they doing? Joseph has shared George's letters with me, and it is clear he still misses your mother, even after all these years."

"He does." Darcy nodded slowly. "But, he rallies for me and Georgiana, at least when we are near. He has told me he wishes my sister to stay home with a governess for another year or two, and I think that is because he is lonely. Though he only sees her two or three times during the day, I suspect that just knowing she is there is helpful to him."

Theodosia patted his hand. "I am certain you are correct." She tilted her head for a moment. "I understand he has been ill recently?"

Darcy sighed. "Yes, he has. I wished to remain at Pemberley with him, but he insisted I attend your house party." He shrugged. "I could not defy him, though I dearly wished to."

"I am sorry. You are in a difficult place, I think. You are a man now and could take over if he needed assistance, but you are not so far from the schoolroom that you feel comfortable ignoring his orders."

"That is it exactly." Darcy felt the tension inside him loosen just a bit. Being understood was a relief.

"I do not want you to worry about him while you are here. You are to have fun, ride with the gentlemen, and perhaps flirt with some girls. Do you understand me? He wanted you to have some enjoyment, and enjoyment is what you will have."

Darcy was not so sure about the flirting with girls aspect of it, but dutifully replied. "Yes, ma'am."

"Good." Theodosia's attention was drawn by sounds at the doorway. She rose, and Darcy joined her, turning so he faced his uncle and Andrew, who had entered the room together.

"Feel better, Cousin?" Andrew approached with a smirk.

"I do." Darcy chuckled. "Though the distance from London to Netherfield was not great, the roads between here and there contain enough dirt to fill all of England."

The young ladies and Frederick joined them just then, followed by a maid and footman with a tea service and platters of meats, cheeses, and bread. The repast was laid out on the low table in front of Theodosia's sofa while the children arranged themselves on various chairs and other furniture about the room.

Darcy watched in silence as his extended family partook enthusiastically of the meal. Though he replied readily enough and consumed more than his fair portion of the food, he was unused to the noise and dramatics involved with such a large group of people. His natural tendency in such situations was to withdraw into himself, and this occasion was no different. However, he did feel welcomed and accepted, which went a long way toward easing his natural reticence.

~~~***~~~

The next day, Darcy joined his uncle, male cousins, and the three male guests who had recently arrived at the party in some sport. Though they would have preferred hunting, there were no rabbits to be found and birds were out of season. A fox hunt was planned for a few days hence, and Joseph preferred the gentlemen wait for that rather than shooting any now. Therefore, the sport largely devolved into impromptu horse races through the fields behind the house. Hours later, the group returned to find the ladies of the neighborhood taking tea with those of Netherfield Park.

Darcy joined the other men in slipping up to their rooms. He removed his riding clothes, washed up using the warm water Smith had waiting in a ewer on his dressing table, and then dressed again in fashionably tight breeches, shirt, waistcoat, and tail coat. Finally ready
~~~

to face the ladies, he trotted down the stairs, meeting the other gentlemen at the bottom.

As Darcy entered the drawing room, his gaze swept the guests. Immediately, he identified the ladies of the neighborhood. He approached with the other men, bowed, and retreated to the window, as was his wont in such situations.

A fresh tea service had followed the gentlemen into the room, and as his aunt began to prepare the pot, Darcy listened to her speaking to the guests.

"I hope you are prepared to enjoy yourselves. I am certain the neighborhood has never enjoyed a house party before like the one we have planned." Theodosia's voice had a tone to it that Darcy had never heard from her before, though he *had* heard it from an aunt on his mother's side, Lady Catherine de Bourgh. It startled him to hear the kind Theodosia Darcy speak so.

"Oh, we have never been invited to a house party here. It has always been single gentlemen who have leased the place before, and they did not host parties for the neighborhood."

Darcy's eyes examined the speaker, a woman about his aunt's age who was dressed in a gown nearly smothered in lace.

"Mrs. Bennet is correct." Another of the ladies, this one in a similar gown to the first's, backed up her friend's statement. "I remarked on it to Sir William just this morning."

"Thank you, Lady Lucas. I confess I am pleased to hear it, for it will be nearly impossible for my party to be unsatisfying when there have been no previous events with which to compare it."

Darcy accepted a cup of tea from Grace, who was assisting her mother. He smiled at her and nodded, but did not speak. His cousin returned to Theodosia's side, and he began to examine the other ladies. On one side of the woman identified as Mrs. Bennet was a girl with similar coloring to his cousin. She sat primly without speaking, a small smile seemingly permanently attached to her face.

On the other side of Mrs. Bennet was another girl, younger than the first and with dark hair instead of blonde. Where Miss Bennet, as Darcy supposed she was called, exuded serenity, this young lady was more expressive. She had blushed when Mrs. Bennet spoke and lifted her cup to take a sip of tea when Lady Lucas talked of Sir William. Darcy tilted his head as he watched her. There was something about her that drew his notice, though he could not put his finger on it.

Suddenly, as though she sensed his gaze, her eyes met his and he was frozen in place. The two stared at each other for a long moment, until a nudge from the older girl sitting on her other side startled her, and she looked away.

Darcy remained still, his heart pounding, as his mind slowly began to function again. He drew in a deep breath, glanced at the intriguing young lady once more, and then examined her companion.

This girl was a few years older than even Miss Bennet. She had dark hair twisted into a chignon at the back of her head. She was dressed similarly to the other ladies. She had an air of sensibility about her.

His examination of the new guests complete, Darcy turned his attention back to the conversation, hoping to learn the name of the fascinating younger girl.

"I suppose, now that the rest of the guests have arrived from their other activities, I should introduce you all." Theodosia did just that. She stood and gestured for the gentlemen and other new arrivals to stand in a line beside her. The ladies across from her stood, as well, and she began to rattle off names, to which Darcy paid close attention.

Miss Elizabeth Bennet. *She looks like an Elizabeth. She is graceful and holds her head high.* Darcy bowed to her when she curtseyed to him. When she rose, her snapping brown eyes met his deep blue ones and, just as before, held for long moments before being forced away as the next lady was introduced.

Chapter 2

Elizabeth Bennet watched the gentlemen enter the room. All were well-dressed and clearly at ease with their companions. They laughed and nudged each other. All except one, who entered at the back of the group. The young man was tall and broad, and solemn. Her heart raced as she examined his features.

Forcing her attention back to her hostess, she just caught her mother saying something outrageous in response to Mrs. Darcy's supercilious question. It was clear to Elizabeth that their hostess thought very highly of herself, and not so well of her guests.

Elizabeth blushed at her mother's words, but when Lady Lucas added her two pence, she had to hide her smirk behind her tea cup. She glanced to the side and gave her friend, Charlotte, a sympathetic look. She looked down at her cup and took a sip when she suddenly felt as though she were being stared at. She brought her eyes up to see the young man she had noticed a few minutes ago. He was looking intently at her, his gaze snaring hers. She could not look away, though she knew she should. It took a poke to her side from Charlotte's elbow before she was able to pull her attention from him.

Elizabeth was relieved when Mrs. Darcy began to introduce the gentlemen. *Finally, I will learn his name,* she thought. She curtseyed to each of the men as they were introduced.

Mr. Fitzwilliam Darcy. *What a funny name! I wonder if it is a family name.* Elizabeth's eyes met his and, as before, held for a long moment. It was only when her friend was introduced that she was able to look away. She watched as Charlotte curtseyed to the gentlemen, but her ears and every other sense were focused on the one she had just been introduced to.

When everyone had been made known to each other, they resumed taking tea, finishing off the meats, cheeses, and cakes, as well as two pots of Mrs. Darcy's favorite tea. When the servants had taken the trays away, Theodosia rose and spoke to the guests. "I will have the housekeeper show you to your rooms. Take some time to settle in. More people will be arriving this afternoon, and I have no activities scheduled except for dinner. The house, gardens, and stables are open to you. Feel free to make yourself at home."

The guests had risen when their hostess did. With a flurry of thank yous and other comments, the ladies of the area bustled out of the room, herding their daughters before them.

Mrs. Bennet and her girls were given a suite in the guest wing of the house. The matron took possession of one bedchamber. Jane and

Elizabeth took the other. There was a shared sitting room between them, with a small dressing chamber attached to each bedroom.

The three were soon settled into their new accommodations and were exploring each other's rooms, admiring the fine furnishings and beautiful décor. A maid appeared not long after, who informed them she had been assigned to them and offered to fetch warm water for washing.

"That would be wonderful, yes. Bring two … Jane and Lizzy can share."

The maid curtseyed and left to complete her task.

"What shall we do after we wash? We shall have hours until we need to change for dinner." Mrs. Bennet clasped her hands together.

"We could walk the gardens," Jane suggested. "That will appease Lizzy's constant desire for movement but be easy enough that you and I can enjoy it, as well."

"That would be ever so lovely!" Elizabeth looked at her mother, willing her to agree.

"Hmmm." Mrs. Bennet thought for a moment. "You know, I have not seen the gardens here in years. I think walking through them is a delightful idea." With a nod of her head, she smiled. "We can wander to our heart's desire and then come back here for a rest before we change."

Smiling at each other, Jane and Elizabeth agreed with their mother. The three then sat to chat and wait for the maid to bring the water.

Within thirty minutes, the water had appeared and the ladies' ablutions had been completed. They exited their sitting room as a group and walked toward the top of the stairs.

"Miss Elizabeth."

A deep voice calling her name made Elizabeth stop and turn towards it, as did her mother and sister.

Fitzwilliam Darcy strode up the hall from the opposite wing of the house. "Mrs. Bennet. Miss Bennet." He bowed. "Miss Elizabeth." Her name came out of his voice as almost a caress, and she sighed inside.

"Good afternoon, Mr. Darcy." Mrs. Bennet greeted him and curtseyed.

"Good afternoon. May I escort you downstairs?" Though he spoke to the mother, his eyes darted back and forth between her and Elizabeth.

"We were going to walk in the gardens." Elizabeth blushed as she blurted out their destination.

Darcy smiled. "I have yet to see them myself. I have been too busy with my cousins and uncle. Might I join you?"

"Why, that would be wonderful! Of course, you may." Mrs. Bennet beamed up at him as her daughters murmured their agreements.

"Excellent." He held one elbow out to the matron, who promptly tucked her hand under it, and one to Jane. Elizabeth smiled and followed. *I wish I had been able to hold onto him,* she thought.

The group made their way down the grand staircase, with Mrs. Bennet chattering the entire way down. Elizabeth blushed brightly at her mother's often intemperate speech. She hoped Mr. Darcy would be able to recognize the excitement behind the endless stream of words and not judge them all by the content. She could tell by the manner in which the other Darcys treated her, her sister, and her mother that they disliked her and her family. She prayed that this one was not that way.

Finally, they reached the bottom and retrieved their bonnets and hats from a servant stationed near the stairs. Then, they walked out the front door and around the side of the house. Elizabeth was pleased to note Darcy extricating himself from her mother's clutches and waiting for her.

"Miss Elizabeth." Darcy bowed and held out his arm to her. "May I escort you around the garden? It is only fair, since I accompanied your mother and sister outside."

With a bright smile, Elizabeth tucked her hand into the crook of his elbow. A tingle travelled up her arm and to her heart. She turned a startled look up at his face, but he only smiled at her. She could not determine if he had felt the same spark she had. "Thank you, sir." She paused. "I hope my mother did not offend with her words. She is thrilled to be here, attending a house party. It is a new experience for her, and she is rather enthusiastic about it all."

She heard Darcy chuckle, a rich, deep, warm sound that felt like being wrapped in a favorite blanket on a cold day. She glanced up at him when he began to speak.

"I thought she might be. She said nothing that cannot be forgiven."

Elizabeth heaved a sigh. "Good. I hope that continues, but you should know that she has her heart set on Jane making a match during the party. She may be too excited now to think upon it, but rest assured, it will eventually occur to her."

"I will be vigilant, I promise." Darcy paused. "What about you? Does she not wish for a match for you, as well? Or, does she wish for Miss Bennet to marry first?"

Elizabeth laughed. "I do not think she cares who marries first." She looked up at her partner again, briefly. "I think she assumes my sister will, but if I were to receive an offer, she would be very happy."

Darcy was silent for a moment, and when he next spoke, he seemed to want to change the topic a bit. "Tell me more about yourself. Do you have more sisters?"

"I do. I have three younger than me. Mary is my next sister, and she will be out next year.

After her comes Kitty, and Lydia is the youngest. Kitty is two and ten, and Lydia is ten, so they must wait a few years to make their debuts." She glanced up to see Darcy nod.

"I have a sister, as well. Her name is Georgiana. She is the same age as Miss Lydia."

"Do you have no brothers?" Elizabeth tilted her head and looked at him again.

"No; none that lived, anyway. My father tells me a brother was born two years after me, but he passed away before his first birthday. My mother lost several before they were born, as well, as I understand it."

Elizabeth's brow creased as she listened. "How awful for you all! Does your mother still grieve them?" She saw Darcy shake his head.

"My mother passed away when my sister was but two years old. A sickness swept through the area and everyone at Pemberley caught it. Mother was always of a delicate constitution. She could not shake it off the way the rest of us did. She died, as did several staff members and many from the tenant families." He paused. "She is missed. I was four and ten; it devastated me. It devastated all of us, I think. My father also misses her deeply."

"I am so sorry!" Elizabeth did not know what else to say. She remained silent, as did her escort. Eventually, Darcy himself broke their silence.

"What do you do for enjoyment? Do you like to read?"

"I do! My father allows me access to his library whenever I wish it. I have read almost every book he has." She paused. "Do you?"

"Very much so. I was reading in the carriage on the way here from London. What do you like to read most?"

"I like everything, to be honest. If I had to choose, I would say Shakespeare's works are my favorites, but I am perfectly happy reading a treatise on agriculture if that is all that is available."

"I confess to being the same. I have yet to meet a book I did not like." Darcy chuckled. "Do you have a favorite from amongst Shakespeare's collection?"

Elizabeth tilted her head as she thought. "I love history, and I love to laugh, so I will say my two favorites are his histories and his comedies. If I were forced to choose just one, I would be hard pressed."

"The histories are my favorite. I enjoy the comedies and tragedies, as well, but there is something about his histories that grab my attention and refuse to let go."

Elizabeth nodded. "I know what you mean." She sighed. "What I like about history, and the reason I like Shakespeare's so much, is learning what people thought and felt." She shrugged. "I am inquisitive, I guess, about the people involved more than the events. I would love to be able to travel back in time for short periods and experience things. What was it like to be a farmer's wife during the War of the Roses? What was Henry the eighth truly like?" She shrugged again. "I am foolish, I suppose. Dry facts bore me, but I am fascinated with how people lived in earlier times."

"I know what you mean. I used to frustrate my tutors with questions such as those. I remember when my cousins from my mother's side visited one summer, and we had all been learning about the Greek and Roman empires. We built a model of Rome and set it on fire. Richard played his violin while we watched it burn."

Elizabeth laughed, her hand over her mouth. She came to a stop, forcing Darcy to do the same. "You set it on fire? What happened then?" She watched in fascination as her companion blushed.

"My father's steward found us. His son was involved in the escapade, you see, and he had been searching for him so he could complete his chores for the day. The fire was mostly out by that point, and we had built it close to the stream so that if the worst happened, we had a water source nearby, but Mr. Wickham lectured us severely. He took his son by the ear and dragged him away. My cousins and I hoped that would be the end of it, but once he put George to work, he went up to the house and informed my father and uncle." Darcy shook his head. "We all got a whipping and had to clean the stables every day for a week."

Elizabeth stared at him, fascinated by his tale. She lowered her hand, her eyes sparkling to match the bright smile she wore. "I am shocked." She giggled, then began to walk once more. "Did you ever attempt such a thing again?"

Darcy laughed. "Nothing that elaborate, no. We did re-enact a few battles now and then, but never anything that would get us into trouble."

"Oh, my!" Elizabeth joined him in laughing. "What a story you have to tell your children one day!"

Darcy smiled and looked down at the ground. "Indeed." He glanced at Elizabeth. "Have you ever done anything similar?"

"Oh, yes, actually, I have. If you ask her, my mother will tell you all about how I vex her on purpose." Elizabeth smirked. "I used to play with the boys of the neighborhood, you see. Playing pirates was a favorite way to pass the time. We would choose the biggest tree we could find that had branches low enough we could climb it and make it our ship. Then, we chose a captain to man it, and he or she chose a crew member or two. The rest of us were the pirates. One was elected the head pirate ... usually me and usually I chose to be called Blackbeard. Then, we fought to overtake the ship with cutlasses made of branches. It was quite fun." She threw a cheeky smile at her escort.

Darcy laughed. "Did you often win this game?"

"Oh, yes. Why do you think I was usually elected head pirate?" She raised a brow.

By this time, they had made a complete turn about the garden, following Mrs. Bennet and Jane as they wandered up and down each path and around all the curved bits and corners. Elizabeth's mother stopped, fanning herself. When Lizzy and Darcy caught up, they inquired as to what was wrong.

"Nothing is the matter," Mrs. Bennet said, which assured Elizabeth that she was well. "I am only tired, and by the look of the sun, we should perhaps go in and begin to prepare to dine. It would not do to be late."

Elizabeth's heart fell. She had been enjoying her discussion with Darcy. She watched as he pulled his timepiece out of its pocket.

"You are correct, Mrs. Bennet. It is, indeed, time to go in and change. May I escort you all back in?"

"That would be lovely. Thank you, sir." The matron turned to her eldest daughter. "Come, Jane. Give me your arm. Mr. Darcy has done such a good job of keeping your sister out of trouble that we shall allow him to accompany her inside."

Elizabeth rolled her eyes before thinking, then blushed a deep red to see Darcy smirking at her. He offered her his elbow once again, and upon taking it, she felt that same spark travel up her arm to her heart.

Chapter 3

Once Darcy had left the Bennet ladies where he had found them, at the top of the staircase, he retired to his rooms. His valet was not quite ready for him, so he wandered back into his bedchamber, untying his cravat as he went. He thought about Miss Elizabeth Bennet, smiling at the memory of her animated conversation.

"It has been a long time since I have spoken so freely to a young lady," he murmured to himself. "Between my studies and their ridiculous conversations, I have avoided the female sex as much as I could. But, she is different." He thought about her open countenance and lack of artifice. "She is young," he said to the room, "but so am I. We could grow together."

Darcy shook his head at his thoughts and the direction they were taking. He had just met the girl. He should not make plans just yet. He thought about how his heart raced at her touch, and the frisson that had shot up his arm each time she had tucked her small hand into the crook of his elbow. "And that was with many layers of clothing between us!" He sighed and smiled to himself. "I will write to Papa about her and get his advice."

Darcy could hear his father's voice in his mind, telling him the story of how he met Lady Anne Fitzwilliam when she was six and ten and knew immediately she was the woman he would marry. He bit his lip as he thought. "Yes, I will write to my father." He headed toward the portable writing desk that was set up on the table near the window.

"Excuse me, sir. I am ready for you now." Smith lowered his gaze in deference to his employer.

"Very good." With a glance back at the writing desk, Darcy turned to go into the dressing room. "I will compose my letter later."

As Darcy began to remove his clothing, Smith drew his attention.

"Excuse me, sir; I did as requested and paid attention to the gossip belowstairs."

Darcy immediately gave the valet his attention. "What did you learn?"

"The talk was mainly about the two families who arrived today, the Lucases and the Bennets. Both families were spoken of warmly. They are apparently the eminent families of the neighborhood. Sir William was knighted by the king a few years ago, when he was Meryton's mayor. He gave up a trade at that point and purchased a small estate, called Lucas Lodge. His eldest daughter is two and twenty, has a small dowry, and no prospects." As he spoke, Smith poured warm water from the ewer into the bowl and handed Darcy a bar of soap.

"I would imagine that is why they are here, then, to try to match the daughter up." Darcy soaped his face and neck, then splashed water over them to rinse them. He accepted the towel his valet handed him and began to dry off. As he straightened from his bent position, he asked another question. "What about the Bennets? Did you hear anything of them?"

Smith nodded briskly. "I did. Miss Bennet is said to be the most beautiful young lady in the county. She is thought very well of and spoken of as calm and kind. Her sister has not been out in society long, but I heard a story or two about escapades she was involved in as a child that made me chuckle. She is also spoken of as kind and tenderhearted."

"That matches what I thought of her." Darcy handed the towel back to his servant. "Anything else?"

"It was mentioned that Mrs. Darcy believes it is wrong for the younger Bennet girl to be out in society. She has stated that Mrs. Bennet is a poor mother for allowing it." Smith held out a clean shirt. When his employer took it, he continued his tale. "Most of the staff lives in the area. They take offense at outsiders speaking poorly of the residents." He shrugged.

"Yes, I would imagine so. Was there anything else said? Perhaps of Mr. Bennet?"

"Ah, yes. There was. Mr. Bennet became master of his estate not long after his marriage. He does not appear to take more interest in it than is required to keep it running. It does well and provides for the family, but some of the staff believes it could yield more if more effort was put into it. It is entailed, according to the cook, who thinks the man does not apply himself better to it because none of his children will inherit. There was some bad blood between the heir and Mr. Bennet, but no one had details."

"So, he is indolent, at best?" Darcy tucked his shirt tails into the trousers Smith had handed him.

"Yes, sir, that is how it appears."

"I saw nothing in the behavior of the three Bennet ladies to indicate bad breeding. Mrs. Bennet is excitable, but in the past I have seen other ladies who were."

Smith held up a finger. "I nearly forgot. Mrs. Bennet's father was the solicitor in Meryton while he lived. Her brother chose not to follow in his father's footsteps and instead, took up a trade and lives in London. Her sister married her father's clerk and that man inherited the business."

"That explains my aunt's dislike. If I were a gambler, I would bet my allowance that she thinks the Bennets are too low because of their connections." Darcy thought a moment while his man tied his cravat. "You mentioned Miss Lucas' portion being small. Was anything said about that of Miss Bennet or Miss Elizabeth?"

"It is believed to be not much more than Miss Lucas', as I understand it." Smith paused, tongue between his teeth, as he focused for a moment on the knot he was tying. Then, having gotten it as perfect as he was capable of, he cocked his head, adjusted the lay of the tail, and turned to pick up Darcy's coat.

"Hmm." Darcy turned and stuck his arms into the coat's sleeves. He shrugged into it, then buttoned it. "Good work, Smith, as always. Please do keep an ear out and let me know of anything else you learn." He glanced at the clock on the mantel. "I have a few minutes before I need to go down. I have a letter to write. I will require you to post it as soon as possible. I will leave it on the table in my room."

Smith bowed. "Very good, sir," he murmured.

Darcy nodded, turning on his heel and striding into the bedchamber. Seating himself at the table, he opened the writing desk and took out paper, ink, and a pen and began composing his letter. When finished, he sanded it, folded it, addressed the back, and applied sealing wax to it. He tapped it on the table a couple times, wondering what his father's response would be. Then, he closed up the ink and put his materials back into the desk, leaving the missive on the table for Smith to find. Rising, he pulled his waistcoat down and straightened his lapels, then exited his room, eager to see Elizabeth again.

~~~***~~~

This time when Darcy reached the top of the staircase, it was not the Bennet ladies he happened upon. Instead, it was his cousin and aunt. He bowed to them before offering his arms to them.

"Thank you, dear." Theodosia hooked her left hand under his right elbow. "Joseph and Andrew were late getting in from whatever it was they were doing and will not be down for a while yet. Grace and I appreciate your escort."

Darcy took a step down, a lady on each arm. "I am happy to be of service. Have the guests all arrived?"

"All but four. Mr. Roger Martin and Judge and Mrs. John Pierce and their daughter are due in tomorrow. Mr. Martin was delayed by a summons from his father, and Judge Pierce had one final case to hear before he could leave London."

Darcy nodded. "Hopefully, the weather will remain fine and they will not have trouble with muddy roads."

"That is what makes summer house parties so attractive." Theodosia raised a brow as she smiled.
~~~

Darcy chuckled, as did Grace. By this time, the three had reached the bottom of the stairs. The ladies let go of Darcy's arms.

"We must check the dining room. Go on ahead and join the others in the parlor. We will not be long." Theodosia stood on her toes to kiss Darcy's cheek. "Thank you."

"I am happy I could be of service." Darcy bowed to his aunt and cousin, smiling as he watched them stroll away. Once they were out of sight, he walked across the entryway to the formal drawing room. There, he found his uncle and cousin standing near a window. He joined them, casting a quick glance around as he did so. He was disappointed that the Bennets had not already come down but pushed the feeling away so he could focus on his relatives.

Joseph and Andrew appeared to be eager to introduce Darcy to the gentlemen who had arrived. So, though he knew the moment Elizabeth entered the room, he was prevented from going to her. The time flew by, however, and almost before he knew it, his aunt was informing her guests that they could forgo being formally seated and that they should sit where they chose.

Darcy looked around and, seeing Mrs. Bennet and Jane being escorted by an older gentleman with graying hair and Elizabeth trailing behind, strode across the room as fast as he could and still maintain decorum. Reaching her side, he smiled and offered her his arm. He drew in a swift breath when a tingle shot up from the point where her fingers touched him to his heart. Exhaling softly, he resisted the urge to lay his free hand over hers and instead, began walking out the door and down the hall.

In the dining room, the couple chose seats together in the middle of the long table. Elizabeth's friend, Charlotte, was on the other side of Darcy, and a gentleman introduced as Sir William Lucas sat on Elizabeth's other side.

As the first course was being served, people began to converse less as a group and more with those to their immediate right and left. For Darcy, that meant his attention was largely focused on Elizabeth.

"Shall we continue our conversation from the garden, Miss Elizabeth?" Darcy tilted his head as he listened for her response.

"That is an excellent idea, sir." She paused in the act of lifting her spoon to think, her head cocked and her eyes twinkling. "We have already spoken of our sisters and our childhood escapades."

"And books."

"Yes, and books." She sipped her soup and swallowed. "What about music? Do you like it? Do you play?"

"I do like music, and I did learn to play the pianoforte, to please my mother, but it has been many years since I have practiced." Darcy dipped his spoon in his bowl. "What about you?" He sipped as he watched her out of the corner of his eye.

"I also play the pianoforte, though not well. My sister, Mary, is already more proficient than I am, and she began to learn after I did. I never learned the harp or any other instrument, sadly." Her bowl empty, Elizabeth placed the spoon within it so the footman could remove them both together.

"Do you practice?" Darcy mimicked her action with his spoon.

Elizabeth smirked. "Not as often or as long as I should."

Darcy laughed. "I was that way when I was learning, as well." He paused as his partner chuckled. "My cousin, Richard, learned the violin, as I told you before. His brother, the viscount, learned the cello."

"So, you had an orchestra, did you?" Elizabeth grinned.

"Nearly so. Richard's two sisters play the harp and the lute, and we did have to perform with them when our parents insisted on showing our skills off for guests, but we only played when forced, except in the burning of Rome incident I mentioned earlier."

Shaking her head, Elizabeth leaned back so one servant could take her soup dishes and another lay out her plate for the next course. "None of us have ever played together, but since only Mary and I play, and we both use the same instrument, it is quite reasonable that we would not. Unless we played a duet, which we have not to this point."

"Miss Bennet does not play?"

Elizabeth shook her head. "No, Jane has never been much interested in music. We were not forced to learn if we did not wish to, and she did not wish to. She professes to enjoy listening to performances but has no desire to perform herself."

"I am surprised your governess did not push her."

"Oh, we never had a governess. We are encouraged to learn what interests us, and masters are made available if we request them, but no one is forced to learn more than basic reading, writing, and number calculations. Mama has undertaken to teach us how to manage a household, of course." Elizabeth twisted her features into a grimace. "Sadly, that includes sewing, embroidery, and knitting."

Darcy laughed at her clear distaste for needlework. "Would that my parents had been that free-thinking." He shook his head. "I had a governess until I was eight or so, at which time my father hired tutors. I went to Eton a couple years later." He shuddered. "I hated that, though I made some good friends there."

"Did you go to University? I should have loved to attend." She sighed.

"I did. Cambridge. I recently completed my course of study there." Darcy looked at Elizabeth out of the corner of his eye as he lifted his fork. "Do you enjoy learning, then?"

"I do. I think that is the normal course of things when one loves to read. It is a shame that females cannot experience higher learning, but Papa has taught me everything he knows, so I feel as though I have almost gone up."

Darcy nodded. "A university education is important for a gentleman, though there are ladies I know who are far superior in intelligence than some of the men of my acquaintance." He shrugged. "It is not a popular opinion, but I think it is a shame that women are not educated better than they are."

"My father has said much the same. My mother, however, despairs of me. She thinks I am ruined by the education I have received. I work as diligently as I do at what she tries to teach me for a reason: to show her I am not."

Darcy could only see the side of Elizabeth's face, but he could tell that her jaw was clenched. His brow creased. He did not like that she was upset and he wondered at her mother claiming such a thing. "Like many gentlemen, I prefer an intelligent wife. Insipid and stupid ladies abound and can be pleasant companions, but I would not wish to spend the rest of my life bored because I married one of them. I would much rather have a rational and intelligent wife." He was heartened to see Elizabeth relax and smile.

"Thank you for sharing that, Mr. Darcy. That is useful information that I am happy to have."

Chapter 4

The longer Elizabeth spoke to Mr. Fitzwilliam Darcy, the more she liked him. She had not spoken to many gentlemen, as she had not been out more than a few months, but he was the first who had talked to her as though she had a brain in her head. Most of the men she had made the acquaintance of so far had made it clear that they did not appreciate her education. She brought her focus back to her dinner partner.

"I am happy to have been able to provide it."

The couple was silent for a short while, as they consumed their meals. Then, the partners on the other sides of each commanded their attention for a bit. Finally, though, they were able to turn back to each other as the dessert course was served.

"Will you take a Grand Tour?"

"I plan to, yes, in the spring of next year. I will leave in April and be gone most of the year." Darcy paused. "Or at least, that is the plan at this time."

Elizabeth nodded, uncertain of what to say. She was happy for his opportunity, but realized that if he were to be gone for the better part of a year, she might never see him again. The thought was too depressing, so she pushed it out of her head and changed the subject. "Do you like attending the theater?"

Darcy smiled. "I do. I try to go to at least one play whenever I am in town. Do you?"

Elizabeth nodded. "I do. I have only gone twice, both times with my aunt and uncle from town, when I was visiting them. They take us at least once per visit. I should like to attend an opera, as well, but Uncle Gardiner dislikes opera and refuses to take us." She giggled.

"Opera is an acquired taste. I do not blame your uncle one bit for not wishing to take you."

Elizabeth grinned and opened her mouth to reply when she suddenly realized that Mrs. Darcy had risen and invited the ladies to follow her to the drawing room. Disappointment stabbed at her, and she could hear the regret in her own voice as she stood. "Perhaps we can finish this conversation later, sir."

As with all the gentlemen, Darcy stood when the ladies did. He bowed to Elizabeth. "I will make certain of it."

Elizabeth's heart fluttered at Darcy's confident speech. She curtseyed with a soft smile and turned to follow the rest of the ladies out. She grinned at Charlotte, who had waited by the door for her.

"Mr. Fitzwilliam Darcy attends to you quite diligently, Lizzy," her friend whispered as she tucked her hand under Elizabeth's elbow. "And you seem to admire him, as well."

"Oh, I do! He is the most handsome gentleman of my acquaintance, and so charming!" Elizabeth lifted her free hand to cover her heart.

Charlotte chuckled. "He is only charming with you, I fear. I have heard him described by the others as reserved to the point of rudeness."

Elizabeth's brows rose but she said nothing. They had entered the drawing room and she looked around. "Do you wish to sit, or shall we join the group at the pianoforte?"

Charlotte's gaze had followed the same path as Elizabeth's. She tipped her head toward the window, where a small grouping of chairs behind some potted plants made a cozy spot for chatting. "There is a nice place. Let us sit there. We will be afforded a small amount of privacy and will not need to watch our words as carefully."

With a nod, Elizabeth agreed. The pair hastened across the room and settled themselves into chairs located right next to each other. The younger girl immediately took up the conversation where they had left it when they entered the room.

"I have observed that he is quiet. He is often so with me, as well. However, I cannot call that rudeness." She gestured toward the room on the other side of the tall plants. "Look at Jane. She keeps her emotions in check and does not share everything she knows with all and sundry. Yet, she cannot be called rude. Mr. Fitzwilliam Darcy is, I believe, similar to my sister."

Charlotte looked thoughtful for a moment. Finally, she nodded. "I see your point. Jane speaks freely with those she esteems, and Mr. Darcy does the same with you." She paused. "Perhaps there is something about you that draws him out." She raised a brow.

Elizabeth giggled. "Perhaps. He certainly draws me out." She sighed. "I love talking to him. He speaks so soothingly, and his replies are well thought out. I have already learned that when he pauses, his next words will be impactful."

"What have you learned about him so far?"

"Well, that he was a mischievous child, for one thing. If you could only have heard his tales earlier today, when we walked in the garden!" Elizabeth laughed. "I am certain he kept his parents and tutors busy!" She grinned and then continued. "We share common interests, such as reading and music."

"And, apparently, a propensity to do things as children that caused your parents misery?" It was Charlotte's turn to laugh when her friend rolled her eyes.

"So it seems." Elizabeth shook her head. "I think, though, that what I like the most about him is that he has shown me great respect. He says he appreciates educated ladies. The other gentlemen I have met were the opposite."

Charlotte nodded in sympathy. "Yes, I remember Mr. Carlton at the last assembly. He was quite decided in his opinion that ladies should not be allowed to learn anything at all."

Elizabeth rolled her eyes, then pulled herself up, tucked her chin, and mimicked that gentleman's pompous voice. "Ladies are too delicate of mind to handle education with any equanimity. They require the firm hand of a husband or father to do anything but sit prettily. They have no reason to learn to read, write, or do sums. That is what God created men to do."

Charlotte giggled. "You do that so well. You have captured the essence of his presentation and his opinion accurately."

Elizabeth had relaxed her spine when she finished her mockery. Now she smirked. "Thank you." She glanced behind her when she heard her mother say something in a louder voice than she should have, given the circumstances. "I am amazed at Mama. She has not pushed Jane at anyone yet."

"She may be waiting until she sees the rest of the guests. If there is a title to be had, you know she will do all she can to make him see Jane."

With a sigh, Elizabeth agreed. "She will. She has not been *too* mortifying yet, thankfully."

"My mother has promised to step in anytime she sees yours becoming overly excited. She wishes for all of us to be seen in the best light."

Elizabeth squeezed her friend's arm. "I thank her for that. We all deserve to be seen as we are, and not judged by the behavior of our families."

The pair chatted a while longer, until the double doors to the hallway opened, and the gentlemen began to file into the room. From their position, they could see the doorway and so were aware of the men's entrance. They stood, as did all the ladies. Elizabeth searched for Darcy amongst the group. Her heart skipped a beat when his eyes met hers the moment he entered. It then sped up to note him proceeding immediately to the alcove where she and Charlotte stood.

Darcy bowed when he arrived in front of the two friends. "Miss Elizabeth, Miss Lucas, I am happy to have found you again."

The ladies curtseyed to him. "We are pleased you could join us in our little refuge." Elizabeth gave him a soft smile. "Will you sit with us a while?"

"Indeed, I will." Darcy looked at the arrangement of the seats and chose a chair, Elizabeth noted, that was close enough to her and Charlotte to allow for conversation but far enough away to maintain propriety.

She wished he had sat closer but understood his reasons for not doing so. *He shows me respect while still wishing to spend time with me,* she thought. The realization pleased her, for it demonstrated to her that he was an honorable gentleman. She heard Charlotte ask Darcy a question, and that brought her attention back to her friend.

"Have you had much opportunity to explore the area?"

Darcy shook his head. "Not yet, not really. I have gone riding with my uncle and cousin and have explored the park here, and the closest of the attached farms, but I have not been further than Netherfield's borders, sadly. I hope to amend that deficit in the coming weeks."

Elizabeth tilted her head for a moment, then asked, "Are you staying for many weeks? Beyond the length of the house party?" She bit her lip as she awaited his response.

Darcy hesitated a moment, but then gave her an answer. "My plans are not yet fixed. My father wished for me to attend the party, at least, but I am free to stay longer, if I would like to. At the moment, I am inclined to do so."

Elizabeth smiled brightly. "I hope you enjoy the party so much that you decide to stay indefinitely."

Darcy smiled back but said nothing.

The three young people spent a pleasant quarter hour speaking about whatever topic entered their minds. Eventually, the ladies prevailed upon Darcy to allow introductions to their fathers. Those made, they wandered around the room together, speaking to each of the other guests and making plans for the morrow.

Eventually, the guests began to retire in twos and threes. Mrs. Bennet and Lady Lucas were among the first. They were unused to late nights and, after the excitement of the earlier part of the day, expressed to their daughters a wish to turn in for the evening.

Swallowing hard, Elizabeth hung her head for a moment as disappointment swept over her. She knew better than to ask if she and Jane could remain longer. She also knew that her mother may have a strong desire for her daughters to marry as soon as possible, but she had not yet reached the point of desperation. Mrs. Bennet was still a stickler for propriety, at least where Elizabeth and Jane were concerned.

So, Elizabeth bid Darcy a reluctant good night. "Thank you for your time and conversation," she said to him.

"I am delighted to have met you, Miss Elizabeth. Perhaps we may find time tomorrow to speak further." Darcy lifted his lips in a smile that took her breath away.

"I should like that very much." Elizabeth glanced back at her mother, waiting impatiently by the door. "Good night, sir." She curtseyed.

Darcy bowed. "Good night."

Elizabeth backed away, wishing with all her heart she could stay with him forever. Reaching her family, she finally turned to follow them, but just as she walked through the portal into the hallway, she looked back. Seeing Darcy watching her, she smiled, lifting her hand in a brief wave, then stepped forward.

She followed her mother and sister up the stairs. Charlotte and Lady Lucas had already reached the top. Their rooms were near the landing, so by the time Elizabeth took the final steps, her friend was out of sight. She silently walked down the hall to her chambers and into the sitting room.

Mrs. Bennet immediately began to fuss. "I do not know why your father insisted on going back to Longbourn. It is an honor and a privilege to be asked to attend a house party, but he acts as though it is nothing."

Jane did her best to soothe her mother's ruffled feathers. "He prefers his own bed, is all. You must admit, as fine as these are, it will make sleep difficult, being in a new place."

"Well, I suppose it will be." Mrs. Bennet pressed her lips together.

Elizabeth spoke up next. "Someone must stay at home with my sisters, as well. We cannot expect Mrs. Hill or the maids to add that to their duties."

Her mother huffed. "Indeed." She shook her head. "Things will be much easier once they are all out. Then, we may attend events such as this as a family and not be separated from each other." She opened her fan and waved it in front of her face. "I will wish you good night now. See to it that you remain within these rooms." She closed her fan and shook it in her second daughter's direction. "No running down to the library, Miss Lizzy! You will ready yourselves for bed. Even if you do not sleep right away, stay here."

"Yes, Mama. I promise to stay within these rooms." Elizabeth did her best not to roll her eyes.

"Good." Mrs. Bennet nodded once, then turned and strode into her bedchamber.

Jane and Elizabeth made their way into theirs, where the maid assigned to them was waiting to assist them. Once the two ladies were in their nightclothes, they dismissed the girl and climbed into the bed. It was their habit to talk a while before going to sleep, and this day had left them with a plethora of things to discuss.

"Did any of the gentlemen catch your eye?" Elizabeth turned to her side so she faced Jane.

"I liked them all – they are all very gentle-manlike, you know – but none turned my head, if that is what you mean." Jane pulled the sheet tightly over her shoulders. "You seem to have found someone, though."

"Mr. Fitzwilliam Darcy, yes." Elizabeth sighed, a grin growing on her face. "Is he not the handsomest gentleman you have ever seen? And so polite!"

"He is handsome, yes. Far more so than his cousin, I think." Jane thought a moment. "He was polite to everyone, even our mother."

"Yes." Elizabeth sighed dramatically. "He is perfect."

Jane laughed. "Lizzy! Are you implying that Mama is difficult to deal with?"

"You know very well she is." Elizabeth laughed along with her sister. "Any gentleman that can remain composed and well-mannered in the face of our mother's effusions must be a saint. That makes him perfect."

"I concede your point." Jane paused again. "Do you think his family will approve of his attentions to you?"

Elizabeth's heart clenched and she grew serious. "I do not know. Mrs. Darcy behaves as though she is far above us and we are dirt under her shoes. The judge has not really spoken to us, but we are ladies and he is a gentleman and that could be why. Then, there is Mr. Andrew Darcy, who behaves toward us much as his mother does."

"Oh, but Grace Darcy has been very warm and welcoming."

Elizabeth nodded. "Yes, she has. Perhaps she is more open-minded than the rest of her family." She shrugged. "It is early days yet. This could end up being nothing more than an infatuation that will fade with time and familiarity, and it really all depends upon Mr. Fitzwilliam Darcy and his opinions, anyway.

So, I will not worry about it. I will enjoy whatever attentions he bestows on me and pray for the best."

Jane reached over to hug her sister. "I will join my prayers to yours. You deserve to be happy as much as anyone."

Elizabeth hugged Jane back. "Thank you. I love you."

"I love you, too."

Each girl leaned over to the table on their side of the bed and blew out the candle that sat there. They laid back down in the dark. Soon, Elizabeth could hear Jane's breathing slow down and knew her sister was asleep. Turning to her side, she thought about Fitzwilliam Darcy. "I hope this is not just an infatuation on his part," she whispered, "because I am certain it is not on mine." She drifted off to sleep with dreams of a future with the handsomest gentleman of her acquaintance floating in her head.

Chapter 5

Darcy turned from the doorway with a sigh. It was unfortunate that Elizabeth had to retire so early in the evening, but he intended to do everything in his power to spend time with her on the morrow.

"Fitzwilliam!"

Darcy looked up to see his cousin Andrew approaching. He stopped.

"Edgewood, Iverson, Edwards, and I are planning to play a few rounds of billiards before turning in for the night. Why do you not join us?"

Darcy shrugged. "I would enjoy that; thank you."

"Excellent!" Andrew gestured toward the doorway. "I was just heading down the hall to get the table ready. Join me. The others will not be far behind."

With a nod, Darcy turned around and walked beside his cousin. He stopped and remained silent as Andrew paused to speak to the footman in the hall, and maintained his silence when they began to stroll again. He was grateful to his cousin for not trying to begin a conversation. His mind was too full of Elizabeth; he wished to dwell upon her more than participate in inane chatter.

Darcy's peace was not to last, however, as he and Andrew had no more than opened the room when the other three gentlemen arrived.

The next hour was marked by the traditional banter amongst young men, largely marked by commentary about the ladies in attendance at the party.

"Hertfordshire seems to have a plethora of beautiful ladies." Gregory Edwards made his remark as he leaned over the table to line up his shot.

"Too true." Henry Iverson leaned on his cue stick, watching as Edwards struck the ball, which hit its intended target but only spun it away instead of sinking it into the indicated pocket. "No offense to your sister, Darcy, but Miss Bennet is probably the most beautiful creature in the county."

Andrew shrugged. "None taken. She is a beauty. It is too bad the family is so low."

Edwards' mouth fell open as he stepped back to allow his friend to take his turn at the table. "Low? I thought she was the daughter of a gentleman?"

"She is. However, her mother is the daughter of a solicitor and her uncle is in trade in London." Andrew sneered as he spoke. "I believe they said he resides within sight of his warehouse."

Darcy looked toward the wall and rolled his eyes. Biting the inside of his cheek to keep himself from saying something he should not, he pretended to be engrossed in the half-full glass of ale he held in his hand. He looked up when he heard Stephen Edgewood snort from the other corner.

"You may look down on tradesmen all you like, Darcy, but some of them are rich as Croesus. I can name three gentlemen – peers – who have married into the families of tradesmen. Times are changing, you know. We all spend money like it grows on trees in the conservatory and put our estates in danger. The dowry of the daughter of a rich importer of goods spends the same as that of the daughter of a duke."

After a moment of silence, Darcy listened as Andrew defended himself.

"Be that as it may, should we throw over the values of our ancestors to fill our coffers? You can, if you like, but I do not intend to. I am a Darcy, and Darcys marry to raise the family's consequence, not lower it. There will never be such a union in our family. Am I correct, Cousin?"

Darcy took a deep breath. "I intend to marry for love, no matter who the lady's family may be." He paused. "Mr. Edgewood is correct. Times are changing. Pemberley does very well, but we do not spend simply to make ourselves look better than we are. There are many families that do. If they wish for their estates to survive, they need to marry where the money is, unless they are willing to live in poverty." He swallowed the last of his ale and set the glass on the small table beside him. "I am only thankful that I am free to marry where I wish." He bowed. "Good night, gentlemen."

As Darcy strolled out the door and down the hall to the staircase, he noted the absolute silence behind him. He wondered again at his cousin's – and his aunt's – opinions. He shook his head as he ascended the stairs. *Thank goodness my father has not raised me to look down on others*, he thought. *I suppose Andrew and Aunt Theodosia will not support me if I decide to pursue Elizabeth as I wish to.* He reached the next floor and turned toward his rooms. *As long as my father does, that is all the family I need, I guess. I hope he replies quickly!*

~~~***~~~

The next few days passed rapidly. Though Darcy could feel the disapprobation of some of his family members, he could not help spending as much time with Elizabeth as he could. He found himself falling deeper and deeper under her spell. Her wit and charm fascinated him, but it was her kindness toward everyone around her that drew him the most.

Darcy had witnessed this kindness first-hand on the third day of their acquaintance. He and Stephen Edgewood had been escorting Elizabeth and Charlotte around the gardens. There were others in the area, mostly the
~~~

young people. His cousin Grace was escorted by her brother; Jane Bennet was accompanied by Henry Iverson; Susan Jameson was on the arm of Roger Martin; and Gregory Edwards walked with Abigail Pierce.

A group of servants was busily setting up a table so the guests could enjoy tea on the patio. Darcy and Elizabeth became separated from Edgewood and Charlotte by virtue of the fact that they had come upon a tall circular hedge, and Darcy had veered his partner left while Edgewood guided his to the right.

As Darcy and Elizabeth came around, Elizabeth collided with a maid, who had come upon them at a fast pace. The servant was unable to maintain her hold on the heavy tray she carried, and Elizabeth was soon covered in thick icing from the pieces of cake that had been on the tray.

"Oh, miss! I am so sorry!" The frantic maid began wiping food off Elizabeth's gown. "I did not see you there. Please forgive me!"

Elizabeth was quick to ease the girl's mind. "All is well. Do not worry. It will wash." She joined the almost-sobbing maid in cleaning herself up. "Please do not fret. I am not angry."

Andrew and Grace, having apparently heard the commotion, came up behind the servant. "What is this?" Andrew's enraged question made Darcy's brows rise. "What have you done, you stupid girl!"

At his words, the maid burst into tears. "I am sorry, sir!"

Darcy could see Elizabeth's eyes widen as Andrew spoke. She immediately drew the maid close, putting her arm around the girl's shoulder. "It was an accident, Mr. Darcy. Accidents can happen to anyone." She glared at her host's son before her gaze moved to the hapless maid and softened. "Please do not cry. I am not angry, and I will not allow anyone to punish you for something I could have prevented."

"Oh, miss! It is just too much! My mother passed last week, giving birth to my youngest brother. I cannot take time away to mourn, because my father needs my earnings to help pay for someone to care for the little ones. I miss her so much!" The young maid sobbed on Elizabeth's shoulder, and Elizabeth allowed it, rubbing her hand up and down the girl's back.

"There, there," she murmured. "I am so sorry for your loss." She maintained the movement of her hand as she raised her head and addressed Grace. "Miss Darcy, surely your mother would make provisions for such a thing. I know we do that at Longbourn. Can she not take a month to tend to her family and grieve her mother, with pay? If you do not wish to compensate her, I will do it, and I will send a maid from my home to take her place so you are not short of staff."

Andrew began to bluster, drawing Darcy's attention away from Elizabeth and toward his cousin. Therefore, he saw the moment Grace pinched him, hard, and shut him up.

"I will speak to my mother about it, but I am certain she would allow it." Grace let go of her brother's arm and stroked that of the maid. "You are Molly, are you not?"

The girl, whose heartrending sobs had diminished though her tears and sniffles had not, nodded.

"I will take you to my mother and see what we can work out. She is not heartless; I am certain you will find her quite compassionate." Grace hooked her arm with that of the maid and led the girl away.

Darcy watched his cousin and the maid for a moment, but his attention was drawn back to Elizabeth, who had drawn herself up to her full height and was addressing Andrew in a manner as harsh as he had ever heard from her. She reminded him of a warrior goddess of old.

"I have found, sir, that the maxim to treat others as I wish to be treated serves me well, regardless of the rank or circumstance of the person to whom I am speaking. Perhaps that is a lesson that you should contemplate further." With a final glare and a shallow curtsey, Elizabeth turned on her heel and began walking toward the house.

Darcy gave his cousin a hard look, then spun around and took off after Elizabeth. He escorted her to the top of the stairs, thanking her for her kindness to the maid and assuring her of his admiration for her actions. He kissed her hand before he let her go, then followed her with his eyes until she entered her chambers.

Later that day, the housekeeper tracked him down where he sat in the library. In her hand was a letter.

"Mr. Darcy, sir." The housekeeper curtseyed. "This just came for you, by private messenger."

"Excellent." Darcy accepted the missive, passing the housekeeper a guinea for taking the trouble to search for him. He waved her away, then broke the seal on his father's note, unfolding the page and reading silently. A delighted grin spread over his countenance. "Thank you, Father," he whispered. He tucked the letter into the pocket of his coat.

Chapter 6

Elizabeth was disappointed over the next few days to be kept from Darcy's side during the day. She could see from the disappointed glances he cast over his shoulder, every time his friends pulled him away for some activity or other, that he would have rather spent time with her. She knew, however, that he could not ignore the others without causing gossip. She did not wish to be the source of rumors because of a gentleman. It was bad enough that her mother was its target so often.

Happily for her, the attention Darcy paid her in the evenings made up for the deficit. For example, as often as the group played games, he chose Elizabeth as his partner. One such evening highlighted one of the characteristics she most appreciated about him, as it was something she had never before experienced from a member of the opposite sex.

The game chosen on that particular evening was Charades, and Darcy had immediately stated his preference for taking Elizabeth as his partner. By this time, Mrs. Bennet had evaluated the incomes – or potential incomes – of each of the gentlemen and had begun actively promoting Jane to two or three of them, including Fitzwilliam Darcy. She noticed his attentions to her second daughter, something

Elizabeth knew based on the fact that her mother had begun to lecture her about letting Jane have precedence with the gentleman. Knowing her sister was not attracted to any of the men in attendance, Elizabeth chose to ignore Mrs. Bennet's words and allow Darcy to attend her as often as he chose. When he positioned himself at her side for the game, the matron immediately began to hiss at her.

"You must allow your sister to partner Mr. Darcy! I insist." Mrs. Bennet leaned toward her daughter's ear from her position beside her.

"Jane has accepted Mr. Edwards as a partner, Mama." Elizabeth gestured across the room to where her sister sat smiling at said gentleman. If she was hoping her mother would keep their conversation private, she was immediately disappointed.

"I'll have none of your insolence, young lady. I do not care what Jane is doing; she does not know what is good for her any more than you do." She looked across at Jane again and called her eldest over. "Jane!"

The eldest Bennet daughter looked at her sister and mother, quietly said something to Edwards with a smile, and rose gracefully. She glided across the room. "Yes, Mama?"

Mrs. Bennet grabbed Jane's wrist. "Come partner with Mr. Fitzwilliam Darcy. Elizabeth will take your place with the other gentleman."

Jane shook her head. "I would rather not, Mama. Mr. Edwards has sought me out specifically, and I would not wish to hurt his feelings or turn him away."

Elizabeth, who had been listening intently, watched as her sister glanced her way for a moment.

"Besides, Mr. Darcy is not my preference." Jane lowered her voice. "I know that he is rumored to have the highest income, but he does not interest me. You would not have me insult our hostess by causing an argument between the gentlemen, would you? She might make us leave."

Elizabeth's eyes widened at Jane's words. She watched as her mother's did the same. She could almost see the progression of the matron's thoughts.

Mrs. Bennet suddenly let go of Jane. "You are correct. Do forgive me." She waved her eldest away. "Go partner with Mr. Edwards." She turned to her second daughter as Jane walked back to her seat. "Behave yourself with Mr. Darcy. Do not carry on as you are wont to do about incomprehensible things no one else cares about."

Elizabeth was startled when Darcy's deep voice suddenly erupted over shoulder, his tone one of displeasure. She froze as he began to censure her mother.

"Miss Elizabeth never 'carries on,' as you put it. She conducts herself in an intelligent and respectable manner. Her behavior is impeccable. I find her everything intelligent and lovely and I dislike hearing that you do not find her so.”

Mrs. Bennet’s jaw had dropped as Darcy spoke. When it was clear he had finished, she stammered a response. “Of course, she is intelligent. She takes after her father.”

“I do not wish to hear you disparage her again.”

Mrs. Bennet still appeared flustered, but she straightened her posture and lifted her chin. “I would never do that to my own child.”

Elizabeth heard Darcy’s intake of breath behind her but at that moment, his aunt stood at the other end of the room and began to instruct the first couple to perform a charade. She glanced around, hoping no one had overheard the conversation, and was relieved to see that they were far enough away from the nearest group of people that the quiet words should not have traveled to their ears.

“Miss Elizabeth, perhaps we should move to seats a little closer to the performers.”

Elizabeth looked up into Darcy’s face and noted his set jaw and unhappy glare aimed over her shoulder. “Yes,” she quickly agreed. “That is an excellent idea.”

She placed her hand in Darcy’s when he stood and offered it to her, and rose to her feet. She turned to her mother. “We would like to sit closer, Mama. If you wish to stay where you are, I do not mind.” She held her breath as Mrs. Bennet seemed to consider the notion. It whooshed out of her at her mother's reply.

"I am comfortable here." The matron waved her hand as if to shoo her daughter away. "Go ahead."

"Thank you." Elizabeth allowed Darcy to lead her to the other end of the room, to a pair of seats not four feet from Grace and Iverson, who had partnered for this game and were the first to perform.

Though Elizabeth did not have the opportunity to discuss with Darcy his defense of her over the next few days, she did speak to Jane about it that night when they retired.

"I was surprised to hear what you said to Mama about Mrs. Darcy. I have never heard such a thing come out of your mouth in all my life. Did you really believe what you said about her kicking us out?"

Jane blushed and looked down, but a smile played around her mouth. "I did not. However, Mama has been pushing me at two or three of the gentlemen and I wished for an evening to simply enjoy myself. I have told her that you and Mr. Darcy seem to be enamored of each other and that I did not wish his attentions, but she cannot see it." She shrugged. "I suppose I was simply tired of it." She sighed. "It has been an enjoyable party, but I confess I would rather be home at Longbourn."

Elizabeth hugged her sister. "I know. It does wear on a person to be in someone else's home for so long. Thank you, though, for your words, even if they did border on a lie."

Jane giggled. "You are welcome. You seemed to have an excellent time tonight. It made it worth the effort." She joined her sister in laughter. When they had both quieted, she asked, "Do you feel the same as you did before?"

"Oh, Jane." Elizabeth sighed. "I love everything about him. I fear for my heart once we go home. You had walked away and did not hear, but he took Mama to task tonight. She began to speak to me as she always does about speaking ..." Elizabeth waved her hand around to the side, as if to encompass the room. "As I always do, I guess. You know she always accuses me of going on and on and making no sense." When she saw Jane nod, she continued. "Well, Mr. Darcy was close enough to hear her and let her know in no uncertain terms that he did not appreciate it." She sighed again. "I have never had a gentleman defend me in such a manner. Papa only laughs." She hung her head. When Jane reached over to squeeze her hand, Elizabeth pressed it in return.

"I am so sorry. I know it is hurtful to you when she does that. I do not understand why she says those things to you. I suspect it is the fear that no one will offer for you and she will not have enough to sustain you both, should Papa pass away."

Elizabeth made a face. "I suppose. Leave it to you to comfort and defend me while at the same time, vindicating the behavior that hurt me." She shook her head. "You are relentlessly positive."

Jane smirked. "I always have been and likely always will be. You may as well get used to it."

Elizabeth laughed. "You always have the same reply."

"And you always have the same complaint." The sisters laughed together again, but then Jane yawned.

Elizabeth covered her own yawn. "We should go to sleep. I love you, Jane."

"I love you, too, Lizzy. Good night." Jane sat up and blew out her candle.

Elizabeth followed suit. "Good night." Before she knew it, she was asleep.

~~~***~~~

A couple days later, Elizabeth and Charlotte were prevailed upon to describe some of the local landmarks. The young people were bored with walking the gardens and playing nine-pins, battledore and shuttlecock, and archery every afternoon and wanted some variation in their entertainment.

"There is a cave not far from here." Elizabeth turned to Charlotte. "Do you remember when we discovered it?"
~~~

"I do." Charlotte's lips twisted into a wry grin. "I also remember how much trouble we caused by disappearing into it for half a day."

"A cave!" Mr. Iverson clapped his hands. "Is it deep?"

Elizabeth shrugged. "I suppose that depends upon how you define deep. It goes into the hillside for quite a ways before it begins to slope downward. There are a couple smaller caves that branch off of it."

"We should go visit it. We can take baskets of food and have a picnic." Grace turned to her mother. "Please, Mama, will you allow it?"

Theodosia frowned at first, and began to shake her head.

"I agree with our daughter, Mrs. Darcy. We will all go along; nothing untoward will happen. It would be quite a delightful time for everyone." Joseph approached his wife and perched on the arm of her chair, putting his arm around her shoulders and cajoling her. "You know you want to."

Theodosia rolled her eyes at him but then shrugged. "Very well. It would not be my first choice of entertainments, but I can see that my husband is eager to experience it, so we shall go." She held up her hand as her guests began to chatter excitedly. "Tomorrow. We cannot spring a picnic on the cook at the last possible moment. She must be given time to prepare and pack up the baskets."

"Thank you, Mama." Grace hugged her mother, then her father, before rejoining her friends to plan what to wear for the outing.

~~~***~~~

The next day, the guests all gathered in the drawing room. It had been decided that the Darcys would convey some of the guests in their carriage, Fitzwilliam Darcy taking some in his, and Gregory Edwards and Iverson each carrying a lady in their curricles. The Pierces and Jamesons would use their own equipages. They would take any others who required a ride.

Fitzwilliam Darcy immediately asked Elizabeth to join him in his carriage. "I have room for Miss Lucas, as well." He nodded to Charlotte, who was standing next to her friend.

"Thank you. I accept." Elizabeth's broad smile lit up her countenance. She turned to Charlotte. "Will you join us?"

"I will. Thank you." She smiled at Elizabeth and curtseyed to Darcy. "We will need a chaperone, I think. I doubt my mother will allow me to ride in a carriage alone with a gentleman and a younger girl."

Elizabeth sighed. "I am certain you are correct. I hate to think what mine would say." She paused. "As a matter of fact, I would rather someone other than *my* mother be our chaperon." She shuddered.
~~~

Charlotte chuckled. "I will ask mine, then. Shall I do it now?"

"Yes, please." Elizabeth winked at her friend. When the other girl walked away, she turned to Darcy. "Have you ever visited a cave before?"

"I have. There are many such places in Derbyshire, and Pemberley has one near the back of the home farm. My friends and I spent many a day exploring it when we were young."

Elizabeth tilted her head. "Have you ever gotten lost in one?"

Darcy smiled and chuckled, looking down at the hat in his hands for a second and then back up at the lady before him. "No, I have not. The one at Pemberley is not terribly deep and has no outlying rooms. We did, however, spend the night more than once and make up stories about pirates and the treasure they may have hidden there in times past."

Before Elizabeth could reply, Charlotte returned, her mother trailing behind. "Mama agreed to be our chaperone."

Elizabeth applauded. "Excellent! Thank you, Lady Lucas."

"Yes, thank you." Darcy bowed to the older woman. "We wished to observe propriety; your attendance upon us is appreciated."

Lady Lucas blushed and stammered. Elizabeth suspected she had not been addressed so by such a handsome man in years.

"The carriages have been pulled around." Theodosia and Joseph stood in the doorway. She raised her voice to address the guests, who were milling about, forming groups and talking. "We will leave in a quarter hour."

Darcy extended one elbow to Lady Lucas and the other to Charlotte, who shook her head and deferred. Elizabeth took his arm, instead, flashing her friend a grateful smile. She noticed a frown, aimed at Darcy, on her hostess' face as the trio, with Charlotte close behind, walked past her. She bit her lip and looked up, but if Darcy noticed his aunt's displeasure, he gave no indication of it.

Darcy handed each of the three ladies into his carriage and followed them in. Charlotte and her mother sat on the forward-facing seat and Elizabeth was on the rear-facing one. Though she noted his surprise, she was not required to explain it, for Lady Lucas did so herself.

"I find that I cannot ride facing the rear. I never have been able to, as my daughter can attest. You can get up to no mischief sitting right in front of me, so I told Elizabeth she could sit with you. She assures me her constitution can handle the discomfort of traveling backwards."

"I can. I am usually required to face that direction when my entire family travels in our equipage, so I am quite familiar with it." Elizabeth smirked. "I can assure you I will not cast up my accounts in your beautiful carriage."

Darcy shook his head and laughed as he leaned back in the seat and made himself comfortable. "My coachman thanks you, as do I. Nothing makes for a more unpleasant journey than the smell of sickness in one's equipage."

"You are quite welcome." With a pert grin and an arched brow, Elizabeth began a conversation that included all within the coach.

Soon, they arrived at the base of the hill whereon the cave was located. The servants had arrived early, and tents and chairs were already set up. It took some maneuvering, but each equipage was able to disgorge its passengers and retreat back down the road a short distance, where they would be parked and the animals unhooked from their traces to forage for a few hours, until they were called upon to take their owners back to Netherfield.

At the unloading point, Darcy stepped out of his carriage first, turning back to hand down Lady Lucas, and then Charlotte, and finally Elizabeth. He did not let go of her hand, instead, tucking it under his elbow and pressing it tightly to his side. "What shall we do first?"

Elizabeth, always eager to experience new things – and what could be more new than visiting a grotto she had seen before with a handsome gentleman by her side – immediately spoke. "I vote we climb up to the cave and explore first, then eat afterwards."

"I agree with Lizzy. We will work up quite a hunger just climbing up and down." Charlotte gestured toward the opening of the cave, which could be seen from their position.

"Very good." Darcy nodded and then turned to Lady Lucas. "Shall you go with us?"

Charlotte's mother shook her head. "Oh, no. I am not climbing up there. I am no spring chicken anymore." She waved her hands in a shooing motion. "The three of you go ahead. I intend to sit myself down in one of those chairs and visit with the other matrons."

Elizabeth saw Darcy's lips twitch and noted that he, like Charlotte, carefully avoided looking at her. *That is probably a good thing,* she thought as she took her lower lip between her teeth and bit down hard, *because I would start laughing and then Lady Lucas would be offended.* When she thought she could control herself, she looked up to see Charlotte's mother duck her head under the side of the tent and take a seat. She turned her gaze toward Darcy when he began to speak.

"Well then. Shall we go up?"

As one, his companions agreed. Thankfully, the path was wide enough that they could walk three abreast, and so they did, taking the climb more slowly than Elizabeth would have if she were alone. They were the first to enter the cave, which was well lit near the front and darker at the back and in the side rooms.

"It was thoughtful of Mrs. Darcy to send servants and lamps ahead." Charlotte nodded toward the footman standing deep in the back with a light in his hands.

"It was!" Elizabeth agreed with her friend. "I had not thought about lighting, but it will be easier for the ladies to see and not get hurt while they're in here."

"As I understand it, my aunt had a terrible experience as a child that left her with a crippling fear of tight, dark spaces." Darcy glanced toward the back of the cave. "I believe that is why she hesitated to approve this outing."

Elizabeth shuddered. "How horrible for her. I know I should not wish to be stuck in a small place."

"Nor I." Charlotte's agreement was strongly voiced.

"No, I would not like it, either. I venture to say that my uncle will force her to climb up here to see for herself that it is not the same as what she experienced so long ago. He has always been one to make those he loves face their fears and try to conquer them. My father is much the same way, though if the person's dread was too great, he would not pressure them." Darcy escorted the ladies down the slope into the back of the cave and then into a side room. "This is rather large."

"It is. This is the room Charlotte and I sat in that day after we had seen everything we could see. It was so much fun to create stories to go with each of the rooms." Elizabeth sighed at the memory.

After a little more looking around, the three exited the chamber, speaking to the others as they went. They stood for a while just outside opening of the cave and looked down the hill facing it, and out over the countryside.

"Such a beautiful view." Elizabeth sighed. "I generally limit myself to my father's land and Oakham Mount, which also offers a fantastic prospect, but this is so much better. You can see all the way to the turnpike from here."

"Yes, it is gorgeous." Darcy paused. "At least as gorgeous as the ladies of the area."

Elizabeth looked up at his words and blushed at the intense look on his face. "Thank you, sir," she whispered. For a second, when his head began to tilt down, she thought he might kiss her, but then Charlotte said something and broke the spell.

"I am hungry. Shall we make the descent?"

Blinking, Elizabeth stammered a little. She gathered her composure, though, and agreed. "Yes, I am rather famished, as well."

As Darcy started to lead the ladies down the hill, Elizabeth heard shrieking behind her. She stopped, as did her companions. Turning, she noted two of the gentlemen, Martin and Edwards, running toward them, pushing, shoving, and laughing. The path in that area ran along a cliff, where the hill dropped off precipitously.

As Martin and Edwards passed, they bounced off each other and Martin bumped into Elizabeth, who automatically stepped back ... into thin air. She gasped as she felt herself falling, her fingertips sliding off Darcy's arm. She looked up, helpless to stop herself, her eyes locking with her escort's shocked ones. A few seconds later, she landed in the dirt on a ledge. She lay there for a long moment, the wind knocked out of her.

"Elizabeth!"

"Lizzy! Lizzy! Oh, please answer us!"

"Eliza!"

As she began to breathe again, Elizabeth could hear Darcy and others in the party calling her name. She opened her eyes, looking up. She tried to call up to them but was unable to speak.

"Her eyes are open!"

Elizabeth could hear the others speaking to each other above her, but could not make out much of what they said. She tried to move, but everything hurt.

"Do not move!" She heard Darcy's voice. "I am coming to help you."

A few minutes later, he was there. "Elizabeth," he whispered. "Are you awake? Can you hear me?" When she opened her eyes again, he closed his and a look of what she thought was relief passed over his features. She watched as he called up to the other gentlemen that she was alive. Then, he turned back to her. "What hurts?"

"Everything." She moaned the word.

"Can you move your feet and legs?"

She moved her feet from side to side, and then her knees.

"Excellent. Do you have pain in them?"

Elizabeth thought for a moment. "No great amount of it, no."

"Good. Will you allow me to feel for breaks? I will not have to move your gown to do it."

She nodded and within seconds, felt Darcy's hands feeling her legs, first at the ankles and then up to her knees and the outsides of her thighs.

"Your arms?"

She bent her elbows and Darcy examined each of her arms for breaks.

"Can you sit up if I help you?"

"Yes." By now, Elizabeth was eager to move. Despite her pain, which seemed to be centered in her back and hips, every time Darcy touched her, it was as if she had been struck by lightning. A spark immediately leaped from wherever he touched to her heart, and it was pounding out of her chest.

Darcy took her hands and pulled her to a sitting position and into his embrace, his knee behind her to support her back. His head and shoulders hid her from the view of the people who were still looking over the ledge. She felt him kiss her hair. He pulled back immediately. "I am so happy you were not seriously injured. How well are you breathing? Do your ribs hurt?"

Elizabeth shook her head. "Not my ribs, as such, but my back hurts terribly. As long as I breathe shallowly, I am well."

Darcy nodded. "Perhaps you have broken no ribs, then. This is good." He looked her in the eye, one hand brushing down her cheek. "I lost ten years of my life watching you fall down that hill. I am sorry I did not anticipate such a thing and prevent it."

"It is not your fault. It was an accident."

Darcy pressed his lips together. Elizabeth noted his gaze falling to hers and her heart sped up.

"You are too good," he whispered. Then, in the lightest of touches, he brushed his lips against hers.

If Elizabeth thought she had experienced sparks before, she was in for a surprise, because the moment his lips caressed hers, fireworks went off in her blood. She stopped breathing and was aware of nothing but the feel of his soft lips firmly pressed against her own. Finally, after what felt like forever but also not long enough, he moved away, pressing his forehead against hers.

"Oh, Elizabeth. One day ..." He trailed off. Then, he helped her to stand and walk to the edge of the ledge she had landed on and down the hillside to where the path once again met the base. There, the other gentlemen met them. One took her free arm and she was assisted to the tents and into a seat.

Chapter 7

As Darcy helped Elizabeth along the side of the hill, he could not help but hold her tightly to his side. He was relieved that she seemed to be reasonably well. He was also angry at the carelessness of the other gentlemen. He was more angry with himself, however. He felt guilty for not seeing the danger and taking steps to prevent it. As a result of this mix of feelings, he did nothing more than nod curtly to Martin when he took Elizabeth's other arm. Now was not the time for confrontation. He needed to see to the needs of the girl he was falling in love with. He could pound the other man into the dirt later.

As the trio approached the bottom of the hill, Jane and Charlotte rushed forward.

"Lizzy! Are you well?" Jane stopped them, taking her sister's face in her hands and looking deep into Elizabeth's eyes.

"I am well, just a bit sore."

Darcy cleared his throat. "She needs to sit down."

Jane startled, but immediately let go of Elizabeth and stepped out of the way.

Darcy and Martin escorted the younger girl to the closest tent, under which Iverson and Edwards had, just moments before, placed a chair as close to the side nearest the hill as they could. As they held her arms to steady her, Elizabeth lowered herself into the seat. Retaining his hold of her hand, Darcy then began to issue instructions to the servants who hovered in the background.

"She will need a blanket from one of the carriages. She has had a shock and will need to be kept warm. You there ..." Darcy pointed to one of the footmen. "You go." He turned to another. "She will need a cup of tea, as well. Bring some here." He turned back to Elizabeth, stroking her hand. "How are you feeling now?"

"I am happy to be seated." She chuckled a little and then winced. "I am still sore, and I am feeling rather tired."

"Tea will help." Darcy squeezed her hand once more.

Mrs. Bennet rushed to her daughter from out of the crowd. "Lizzy! What have you done now?" She took Elizabeth's free hand and lifted it to her lips. Then, keeping her daughter's appendage in one of her own, she used the other to smooth back the hair from Elizabeth's forehead. "Where are you hurt?" Her eyes raked the girl's form. "Is anything broken?"

Darcy could see the matron's concern for her child. She had not voiced it well at first, but her behavior after the initial outburst was everything he expected from a caring mother. "Miss Elizabeth gave me permission to check her limbs for broken bones. I found none, thankfully. She has owned to some pain in her back, however."

Surprise had flitted across Mrs. Bennet's face when Darcy began to speak, but she nodded when he finished and sighed with what he assumed was relief.

"Good, good. I am glad. Thank you." She looked at Elizabeth. "Do you still have this pain? You are shivering! You need warmed up!" She looked around just as the footman arrived with the carriage blanket. She snatched it from his hands and laid it over her daughter, tucking it in around her.

On the other side of Elizabeth, a cup of tea appeared. Darcy accepted it, handing it to her carefully. "I hope you like your tea plain, Miss Elizabeth, as it appears that is what the footman brought you."

Elizabeth grimaced as she accepted the cup. "I do not, but it will do for now." She took a sip as her mother, now assured her daughter was as well as she could be given the circumstances, began to reprimand her for nearly giving her a heart seizure.

Darcy rolled his eyes and looked away. Noticing the other ladies now beginning to crowd around Elizabeth, he squeezed her hand and gave her a smile before letting go and melting back into the crowd. He stood apart, close enough to hear what she said but far enough away to give her and her friends room. He was relieved to hear her tell them that she did not wish to go home until the outing and picnic were completed.

~~~***~~~

Darcy was even more diligent in his attentions to Elizabeth after her fall than he had been before. He checked in with her in the mornings before going out with the gentlemen and did so again every afternoon when they returned. He wondered if she should have spent a couple days in bed, but she vehemently assured him she did not.

"I hate above all things to be inactive. It is bad enough that I have been forced to limit myself to brief walks about the gardens. I am not about to lie in bed for days at a time. If I did that, I may as well go home." She shook her head so hard, her curls bounced up and hit her cheeks. "No. I will move about as much as I am able."

Darcy pressed his lips together. He was unhappy with her decision but she was not his wife that he could order her around. "I see." He sighed to himself. "Then, please allow others to assist you. I will stay near as often as I can and am quite willing to fetch things for you, and my aunt has plenty of servants who can do the same." He paused and looked her in the eye. "I care very much about you and do not wish to see you in pain. Promise me you will ask for help when you need it."
~~~

Elizabeth tilted her head and gave him a soft smile. "For you, I will make that promise. Besides, I do wish to be able to dance at the assembly on Thursday."

Darcy smiled back. "Will you be well enough, do you think?"

"Oh, I plan to be!" Elizabeth laughed.

"Then, will you save me a set or two?" Darcy longed to hold her hand again. He had enjoyed the feel of it in his the day she fell and wished to experience it again.

"You may have whichever of the sets you like. No one else has asked for any."

Darcy felt relief zip through him. He gazed into her eyes. "The first and last sets."

"They are yours." Elizabeth's delighted smile and twinkling eyes were enough to make Darcy lean forward for another kiss. He caught himself, however, and sat back again, contenting himself with smiling at her.

~~~***~~~

The day of the local assembly was also the last full day of the house party, with the ball being its culminating event. Theodosia had hired a dancing master to come to Netherfield from London for the afternoon. His purpose was to make sure all the attendees' dancing skills were up to par. Darcy was happy to discover that Elizabeth felt better enough to participate in the lessons. He made sure he was the one to part-
~~~

ner her. He noticed the disapprobation of both Theodosia and Andrew, but chose to ignore them in the interests of family unity.

That evening, Darcy was quite proud to lead off the first set with Elizabeth as his partner. They moved through the steps as one, with a grace and fluidity that most in attendance could not manage. He could hear whispers from the sidelines about them.

Elizabeth arched a brow as she stepped around him. "It seems, sir, that all of Meryton expects a match to be made between us."

Darcy smirked at her. "So it seems."

"Is that all you have to say?"

Darcy shrugged. "For now, yes it is." He took her hand to promenade down the line and back up. "I cannot say much as of yet. I know what I wish for, but is it fair to ask a lady to wait nearly a year for me?"

It was Elizabeth's turn to shrug. "I do not know. It might be, and it might not."

Darcy was silent for a long moment. The first dance of the set ended and he returned to his side of the line, applauding politely. When the second dance began and they stepped to the middle he asked the question that was on his mind. "The rest of the guests are leaving in the morning. I have told my uncle I would like to stay on for a few weeks. May I call on you?"

A slow smile spread over Elizabeth's face as the steps of the dance took her away. When she came back, his hopes were answered. "I would be delighted to receive you."

~~~***~~~

Darcy waited a full day after Elizabeth returned to Longbourn to call. He was nervous; he had never called on a lady before and did not know what to expect.

He stood behind the housekeeper as she announced him, wiping his sweaty palms on his breeches.

"Mr. Fitzwilliam Darcy."

He bowed to the ladies as Mrs. Hill exited the room behind him and shut the door. He immediately found Elizabeth with his eyes. "Good afternoon."

The ladies curtseyed and Mrs. Bennet greeted him.

"Welcome to Longbourn, Mr. Darcy. Do be seated. You are our first caller of the day."

Darcy strode across the room toward Elizabeth as he replied. "Thank you. I am happy to be here." When he stood in front of the woman of his dreams, he bowed again. "Miss Elizabeth, I am delighted to attend you today."

Elizabeth's smile went a long way toward relieving his nerves. "I am happy you came over. Will you sit with me?"

"Gladly." Darcy settled himself on the sofa as near to Elizabeth as was possible and still remain within the bounds of propriety.
~~~

"You will get the chance to meet my younger sisters in a few minutes. They should be done with the sums Mama set them to at any moment, and then they will be allowed to greet our visitors."

"Excellent. I remember you have three younger sisters?"

"I do." Elizabeth smiled. "You may have the opportunity to meet my father, as well."

Darcy's brow creased. "I think I have already, at the fox hunt my uncle held."

"Ah, yes." Elizabeth nodded. "I had forgotten about that. What did you think of him?"

"He seems to be rather more intelligent than the rest of the neighbors." Darcy paused. "Not to say they are deficient."

"Oh, no, they are not, but you are correct about my father. He has always loved to read and learn and I fear there are no other gentlemen in the area who share his interests." Elizabeth lifted her shoulders and dropped them. "He has taught me all I know about philosophy and history and geography ... almost any subject I have discovered, he has been able to assist me in learning. He also loves to tease and finds amusement in the foibles and follies of his peers."

Darcy tilted his head. "Interesting." Before he could say anything else, the three youngest Bennets entered the room, two of them noisily and one quietly. The remainder of his visit was filled with responding to questions from the youngest girls and their mother, and he had no more opportunity for discussion with the lady he had actually come to visit.

~~~***~~~

Over the course of the following fortnight, Darcy visited Longbourn almost every day. When he discovered that Elizabeth loved to walk to Oakham Mount in the mornings, he made a point of riding his horse in that direction just after dawn each day, which is when he had determined she was most likely to be taking her exercise. They enjoyed many a chat as they meandered up her second-favorite hill.

On the fourteenth day of his unofficial courtship, Darcy began to descend the staircase dressed to visit Longbourn when someone began to pound on the front door. The nearest footman opened it, and Darcy saw his father's personal messenger step inside. He froze halfway down.

"Express for Mr. Fitzwilliam Darcy." The rider opened his bag and pulled out a letter, handing it to the servant.

The footman accepted the note and turned, stopping when he saw Darcy begin to run down the remaining steps.

Darcy took the note from the servant and looked around.

"The library is empty, sir."
~~~

With a quick look of gratitude toward the man, Darcy turned and hastened down the hall. Entering the library, he strode to the window. The script on the front was not that of his father, and his mind raced. Taking a deep breath, he broke the seal and unfolded the sheet.

21 August, 1805

Pemberley, Derbyshire

Master Darcy,

Please forgive the brevity of this message. Your presence is required immediately, as your father has fallen gravely ill. The physician has been to see him and has told us his time is drawing near. Please come home immediately.

Your servant,

John Wickham

Darcy's heart began to pound as his eyes darted back up to the top of the page. *Father,* he thought. *Dying? No, it cannot be!*

He whirled around, charging out of the room and down the hall at a run. He sped up the stairs, taking them two at a time, and startled his valet when he threw open the dressing room door.

"Pack my bags and order my carriage. We must return to Pemberley immediately!" Without waiting for Smith to respond, he raced into his bedchamber and began to gather his portable writing desk and other things on his bed for the valet to pack.

"Cousin! What is going on?"

Darcy turned, seeing Andrew standing in the open doorway.

"My father is ill. He is dying. I must go to him, immediately."

Andrew stepped into the room. "Of course! I will tell my father. He will send word ahead to the inns for fresh horses. Do you intend to drive through the night?"

Darcy shook his head. "My driver will need at least one night of sleep, but we will not stop for anything else. My father's messenger is probably in the kitchen. I am certain Uncle will be able to send notes with him. He is a faithful and competent courier."

"Very good." Andrew turned to leave.

"Wait." Darcy paused. "Elizabeth." He whirled back to the bed and pulled writing supplies out of the portable desk. He dashed off a quick note to her, sanded it, and sealed it. Then, he turned back to his cousin, holding the missive out to him. "Please give this to her. It tells her what happened and where I am. We were to go for a walk with her sisters today. Send it with a servant if you do not wish to go yourself." He hesitated again. When Andrew finally took the missive from him, he spoke once more. "My father gave me permission in his last letter to court her. He approved of her and her connections. I know you do not like it, but as my cousin, I expect you to put aside your feelings and do as I ask. I would do the same for you."

Andrew said nothing, merely nodding before disappearing through the doorway.

A footman poked his head into the room. "Sir, the coach and driver are waiting in front of the house."

"Thank you. My valet will probably have instructions for you to send whatever is not currently packed along after me."

"Yes, sir." With a nod, the footman stepped out again.

Within a quarter hour, Darcy was on his way, Smith sitting on the seat opposite him. He leaned his head back, worry for his father uppermost in his mind. His heart, though, was full of Elizabeth. He missed her already.

Chapter 8

At Longbourn, Elizabeth paced back and forth in front of the window in the drawing room. It looked out over the driveway, and she was anxiously waiting for Darcy to arrive.

"Lizzy," Jane said, "he will not get here any faster if you are watching for him. Come sit with me. You know Mama will have a fit if she sees you."

Sighing deeply, Elizabeth obeyed. "It is not like him to be late. I hope nothing has happened to him. He promised to walk with us into Meryton today. He always keeps his promises."

"I am sure he is fine. He would send a message if he could not come, would he not?"

"I would think so." Elizabeth twisted her hands in her lap. "My imagination is alive with all the things that could have happened to keep him away."

Jane had no reply to this, so remained silent.

A few moments later, Mary, Kitty, and Lydia entered the room, the youngest two bursting through the door at a near-run and Mary following sedately behind.

"We are ready to walk into town! Come on, hurry!" Lydia grabbed one of Elizabeth's hands and one of Jane's and pulled at them.

Mary looked around. "Where is Mr. Darcy? Is he not to join us today?"

Elizabeth exchanged a look with Jane before she replied. "I do not know where he is. He was supposed to join us, yes. Something must have happened to make him late."

Kitty's fists landed on her hips. "We are not waiting for him, are we? I want to look at the ribbons in the milliner's shop before Maria Lucas purchases the prettiest ones."

Lydia joined her voice to that of her next older sister, and Elizabeth begrudgingly gave in. The five girls made the trek into Meryton, visiting a couple shops and taking tea with their aunt and uncle Phillips.

If anyone noticed Elizabeth's constantly-turning head as she searched up and down the lanes, hoping to see Darcy, they said nothing. When bedtime came and there was no word, she was beginning to despair.

Elizabeth cried to Jane when they talked before bed. "What is wrong? Is he injured? Did he leave me?"

Jane held her sister, rubbing her hand up and down her back. "I am so sorry. I do not know what happened. I would have thought someone from Netherfield would have sent a note. It must have gotten overlooked. Tomorrow we are to go to Lucas Lodge to dine; you know the Darcys were invited. Perhaps Mrs. Darcy or Miss Darcy will be able to give you news of him."

Elizabeth nodded, wiping her eyes and nose with the small square of muslin in her hand. "I hope so."

After a few minutes of further conversation, during which Jane attempted to soothe her sister, they parted. Jane went to her room to retire, and Elizabeth climbed up into her own bed and cried herself to sleep.

~~~***~~~

The next evening, as soon as the Darcys arrived at Lucas Lodge, Elizabeth started working her way through the crowded room toward Theodosia. The house was packed full of people, the Lucas home being small and the guest list including all four and twenty families of the district. When she finally reached the older lady's side, she had to wait for a lull in the conversation. It finally came, and she immediately took advantage of it.

"Mrs. Darcy?" Elizabeth curtseyed. "Good evening."

Theodosia turned from the other women she was speaking to and nodded at Elizabeth. "Good evening, Miss Elizabeth. Are you well?"

"I am; thank you. I was wondering ..." Elizabeth trailed off for a second as a sudden sense of fear overtook her. She shook it off and lifted her chin. "I do not see Mr. Fitzwilliam Darcy here tonight. I hope he is well?"
~~~

Theodosia shook her head, causing the younger woman to gasp. "He was well when he left. He received a message from Pemberley. His father is gravely ill and his presence was required at home. I am sure you understand that his life is far removed from this small hamlet. He is destined for great things, including making a spectacular marriage. We have high hopes for him."

Elizabeth had begun to breathe again as Theodosia spoke. Her mind was racing; she needed time alone to think about what the older lady had said. For now, all she could do was thank the woman for her information, curtsey, and walk away.

As quickly as she could, she found a quiet corner in which to sit. Tucked away as she was beside a large, freestanding china cabinet, she was almost guaranteed a few minutes of peace and solitude. She closed her eyes and pressed her hand to her pounding heart. *He is gone. His father is dying. Poor Mr. Darcy!* She took a deep breath, willing tears away. *I cannot fault him for leaving immediately, even if he did not send me word. Perhaps there was not time.*

Theodosia's words echoed in Elizabeth's mind. *"...a spectacular marriage. We have high hopes for him."* She whispered, "A spectacular marriage. I know she does not mean to me." She bit her lip, hoping to ward off a new surge of tears. One escaped the corner of her eye and she surreptitiously wiped it away with her finger. She wanted to go home. She needed to weep and pray. *Would Mama allow me to leave?* She doubted it. *What about Papa? I could plead a headache.* She swallowed. *No, he would not allow it, either, for then he would be required to listen to Mama's ranting on the morrow. His peace is more important than mine.* She sighed. There was no hope for it. She would have to dig deep for a bit of serenity and plaster a smile on her face. The rest would have to wait until bedtime. The dinner gong rang, and the rest of the guests began to move toward the dining room. She rose to join them.

~~~***~~~

Hours later, Elizabeth dismissed the maid and took her favorite position in the window seat of her bedroom. She pulled her feet up and arranged the hem of her nightshift to cover her toes, then she leaned against the window and allowed the feelings to rise. She began to cry, softly at first, but as Theodosia's explanation began to once again wend its way through her mind, the sobs became more intense.

"Why?" There was no one to reply to her question, but she could not stop the asking. Maybe God would hear her and send an angel to give her an answer. *Or not,* she thought. She cried a little longer, worried about Darcy and grieving his absence. Finally, she moved. *I will write in my journal. That always helps me deal with my feelings.*
~~~

Pulling the small book out from under the floorboard under her bed – Lydia had a habit of sticking her nose into things that did not belong to her, as well as stealing things she wanted, and Elizabeth did not want her journal to become fodder for her youngest sister's dramatics – she picked up her small portable writing desk and settled herself again in the window seat.

Friday, 23 August, 1805

Mrs. Darcy told me today that Mr. Fitzwilliam Darcy was called back to his home, because his father is dying. My heart is broken, both for Mr. Darcy's pain and because I doubt I ever see him again. He left me no messages to assure me of his affections or his return. I do not know what to think of this.

I received this news at a dinner party a few hours ago, at Lucas Lodge. I was devastated, but could not react in public. Instead, I found a seat off by it-self and sat until the dinner gong sound-ed and I was forced to rejoin the party.

To top it off, Mrs. Darcy made it clear that her nephew is expected to mar-ry high. "Very well" is the term she used. It was plain that she did not mean me. I bring very little to a marriage, just one thousand pounds, and that not until my mother passes. I have only myself to offer, and if his family does not approve of me, it will not be enough. I do not wish a marriage like the one I see every day. It would break my heart for him to treat me without respect, the way Papa does Mama. And I would hate myself were I to become a silly woman because of my nerves.

I have not spoken to Jane about this. She was exhausted when we returned home and wished for nothing more than to go to bed, so I did not ask her to talk with me. I am certain she will want to hear it all tomorrow, and that is soon enough. Hopefully, the worst of my initial reactions will be past and I will be able to recount the tale and still retain my composure.

My mind is tortured. I was certain he was as attached to me as I was to him. He asked to call on me here, and extended his time at Netherfield by a full fortnight. He spent part of every single day here at Longbourn, attending to me to the exclusion of everyone else. Is not incivility the very essence of love? He kissed me, and as much as said he wished to marry me. At the assembly, he wondered if it was fair to make me wait a year for him. He danced twice with me! Twice!

If his father does die, I doubt he will go on his Grand Tour. He cannot, not if he is in mourning. I know that will be a disappointment to him. He was eagerly looking forward to exploring the Continent. The thought of it squeezes my heart even harder.

So, here we are. I am in Hertfordshire and he is in Derbyshire, more than one hundred miles away. I will probably never see him again. I know I must accept this, but my rebellious heart completely rejects the notion. What am I to do? I cannot have him, but I cannot live without him. I feel as though I am suffocating. I cannot breathe.

Has anyone ever actually died from a broken heart? If not, I feel that I may well be the first.

Elizabeth wiped the tears that poured down her cheeks, sobbing into her handkerchief for a good long while. When her weeping began to diminish, she blew her nose, put away her writing desk, placed her journal back into its hiding spot, and climbed into bed. Realizing her muslin square was soaked through, she got up again to pull three or four more out of the drawer, then got back under the covers. She cried herself to sleep.

~~~***~~~
~~~

Elizabeth rose late the next morning. Her dreams had been filled with nightmares of Darcy, his father, his aunt, and his rejection of her. As a result, she felt sluggish and out of sorts. She made her way to the breakfast room, making up a plate at the sideboard and taking it to her customary place at her father's right hand. She noticed his concerned look and furrowed brow and waited to see if he commented.

"Are you well, Lizzy? You did not take your customary exercise this morning and you are pale."

"I am well." She gave him a small smile. "My sleep was plagued with horrible dreams." She shrugged. "It must have been something I ate."

She could see that her father doubted the accuracy of her explanation by the deepening frown on his face and the way he paused. Finally, though, he shrugged and went back to his meal. She breathed a silent sigh of relief and started picking at her eggs.

"Good morning." Jane greeted her sister and father as she entered the room.

Elizabeth murmured her reply and kept her focus on her meal. When Jane sat down beside her, placing her plate on the table next to Elizabeth's, the younger girl was forced to attend her sister.

"Are you well? I am sorry I was unable to speak with you last night." Jane kissed her sister's cheek.

Mr. Bennet rose. "I will leave you girls to your discussion. I am certain it will involve gentlemen or lace, neither of which I have a taste for. If either of you need me, I will be in my book room." He gave Elizabeth a brief stare, making it clear to her that he meant her, specifically, and then picked up his paper, bowed shallowly, and left the room.

Elizabeth turned her gaze back to her meal.

"Lizzy?" Jane's brows rose as she looked at her sister for a moment before picking up her sweet roll and taking a bite.

"I will explain later, when we have privacy." Elizabeth tipped her head up to indicate their sisters, who could now be heard abovestairs as they readied themselves for the day.

"As soon as we finish breaking our fasts." Jane's words carried a promise, so Elizabeth simply nodded and turned her attention back to her plate.

Later that morning, the pair locked themselves into Elizabeth's room. Jane once again held her sister as she cried. "Surely he must have sent a note. Perhaps it got lost."

Elizabeth only shrugged. "Perhaps, but that does not matter. I will never see him again. I must get over this. I must move on and set him aside."

"Oh, Lizzy. I am so sorry."

"Thank you. I will be well."

"So you shall, my dear. You will be yourself again. But, promise me you will not jump into another courtship until you have allowed your heart to heal."

Her lips twisted into a wry smile, Elizabeth assured Jane of her compliance. "Never fear, my dear sister. I promise you that I may *never* enter into another courtship again." Truthfully, she did not think she would ever be able to love again, because Mr. Fitzwilliam Darcy held the key to her heart and no one else would do.

~~~***~~~

Though Elizabeth did her best from that point to forget Darcy, he was never far from her thoughts. When she learned at the first assembly in October that Darcy's father had died the week previously, she grieved anew, both in sympathy with him for his loss, and for the loss of their love.
~~~

Chapter 9

Darcy felt the coach slow as it approached the turnoff into Pemberley. Except for a few hours during the night and very brief stops to change horses, they had traveled without stopping since leaving Netherfield the day before. He was anxious to reach his father's side and prayed he was not too late.

Finally, the equipage came to a stop in the courtyard. Darcy flung open the door and leaped out, not waiting for a servant to open it for him. He raced up the steps, stopping short when Mrs. Reynolds, the family's long-time housekeeper, stepped out onto the porch.

"My father?"

Mrs. Reynolds took the time to dip into a brief curtsey before replying. "He is in his chambers. The doctor is with him. He is hanging on for you, I believe." She stepped out of the way and gestured for him to pass. "Go to him. He will be eager to see you."

Darcy stared at the open doorway for a long moment, frozen in his tracks. He listened to the housekeeper's words and swallowed. Finally, he nodded and took off, charging up the stairs and down the long hall to the master's bedchamber. He paused before knocking, straightening his waistcoat and taking a deep breath. He closed his eyes, opened them, and lifted his hand, rapping on the door. He waited for a response, holding his breath.

The door opened. "Come in." Mr. Carter, the local physician, waved Darcy into the room. "He has been waiting for you."

"How is he?" Darcy stepped into the room and stopped, turning an intense gaze upon his father's favorite doctor.

"He is hanging on. I will speak more about it to you later." Carter gestured to the bed. "Go; speak to him so he will rest."

With a sharp nod, Darcy moved toward the bed. He could see his father, covered nearly to his chin, with one arm lying outside the covers. He was shocked at the sight. The elder Darcy had always seemed larger than life, but today, he appeared small, much smaller than he ever had.

"Papa?" Darcy sat in the chair situated at his father's elbow and watched the older man's eyes open.

"Fitzwilliam?" Mr. Darcy's hand moved, reaching for his son.

"I am here." Darcy's words were whispered, because he found himself suddenly on the edge of tears.

"I am happy to see you. Forgive me for pulling you away from Miss Elizabeth." The elder gentleman's lips lifted in a ghost of a smile.

"Think nothing of it. She is a kind young lady. She will no doubt forgive you." Darcy's heart clenched at the thought of her. He missed her terribly.

"Good." Mr. Darcy closed his eyes, breathing heavily. He sighed deeply, then opened his eyes again. "I have much to tell you, to impart to you. Carter tells me my time is short. I have taught you how to run the estate, but there is so much I have failed to share with you about your family and your history, and my hopes for you and your sister."

Carter spoke from the other side of the bed. "You must take time to rest, sir."

Darcy glanced up at the physician and nodded, then looked at his father once more. "I have just come in from the road. Allow me to wash and change and I will come back. I will have tea with you, if you wish."

"Very well," Mr. Darcy whispered. "I could use a nap." He yawned. "I am very tired. Bring Georgiana with you for tea. I have not seen her yet today. I long to hear her sweet voice."

"I will, Father." Darcy stood, leaning over the bed to kiss the older man's cheek. "I will return in a little bit." He stood and stepped back, gesturing with his head for the doctor to accompany him into the hallway.

"Tell me what is happening." Darcy clenched his fists at his side the moment the door shut behind the doctor. "I knew he was ill in London before I went to my uncle's, but he assured me he would be well. I thought he was feeling better."

Carter shook his head. "I do not know exactly what is wrong with him. Based on his symptoms, I suspect a growth in his lungs, a cancer. He often has difficulty breathing, but shows no signs of consumption."

"Cancer?" The word filled Darcy's head with all manner of imaginings. "I was told he will die soon?"

Carter nodded. "I believe so. He has been in a decline for months. His body is worn out from fighting the tumor. As I said before, I think he has only held on this long because he has things he wishes to say to you. In my professional opinion, he will be gone within the month, six weeks at the longest."

Darcy hung his head for a long moment, while the doctor waited quietly. He looked up. "There is no hope, then?"

"No." Carter shook his head. "None. I am sorry."

Darcy took another deep breath and nodded, waving the physician away. He turned to stagger down the hall to his own set of rooms, tears blurring his vision. Once in the privacy of his chambers, he sat in a chair by a window and put his head in his hands and cried.

"Elizabeth," he whispered. "How I wish you were here. Your presence alone would comfort me." He wondered how she had taken his news. "I hope you can forgive me for leaving so suddenly. I wish I could write to you, but we are not engaged." He sniffed. Wiping his eyes with the heels of his hands, he stood and walked to the other window, where a small desk was positioned. He pulled out the chair, seated himself, and prepared a pen and paper. "I will write to your father and ask him to give you a message from me. That will have to do."

Darcy wrote the note, reread it, crossed things out and corrected them, then read it again. Then, he pulled out a fresh sheet of paper and carefully rewrote it. He sanded the clean copy, folded it, sealed it, and addressed it.

"Sir?"

Darcy was so intent in his purpose that Smith's voice startled him. "Yes?" He turned in his seat to look at the valet.

"A bath has been prepared for you."

"Very good." Darcy stood, picking up the letter. He walked toward the dressing room and stopped in front of his personal servant. "This needs to be mailed. It does not have to go by messenger or anything. Send it with the post tomorrow."

Smith took the missive. "Yes, sir."

~~~***~~~

An hour later, Darcy was bathed, shaved, dressed, and rapping on his sister's door.

Miss Fitzhugh, Georgiana's governess, answered his knock.
~~~

"Come in, sir. Miss Darcy is just about ready." Miss Fitzhugh stepped back and curtseyed. "I will tell her you are here."

Darcy stepped into the room, leaving the hall door open. Moments later, his little sister came running toward him. He opened his arms and she threw herself into them.

"Brother! You are here! I am so happy to see you!" Georgiana hugged him tightly around the neck. "I have missed you. Papa has been ill. Have you seen him?" She pulled back and looked at him, a crease between her brows.

"I have. I am come to escort you to have tea with us."

The little girl sagged in his arms. "If he is well enough to have company for tea, it is a good thing."

"It is good." Darcy paused, setting her down and putting his hand on her shoulder. "But he is not well, my sister, and we must prepare ourselves for him to leave us."

Tears welled up in Georgiana's eyes, making Darcy's heart clench. "I know," she whispered. "I am glad you are here with me. I did not want to be alone when it happened."

Darcy swallowed hard and hugged his sister again. "I am here, and I will not leave you. Come, let us go see Papa."

~~~***~~~
~~~

Darcy spent as much of his time with his parent as he could, though the running of Pemberley kept him occupied most of each day. He was grateful his father was still able to approve his decisions and discuss issues with him that he struggled with.

Most often, during his times sitting at the elder Darcy's bedside, father and son talked about the future.

"I have promised Wickham to care for his son. In my will, George will receive a small bequest and the promise of the Kympton living when it becomes vacant, if he takes orders."

Young Darcy shifted in his seat, an action the elder man apparently noticed. "You are uncomfortable with this?"

Darcy hesitated but finally decided just to say it. "Yes, sir, I am. He is the most ill-suited man to hold the position of any that I know. The person he presents himself to be in your presence is not the one he shows to the rest of the world."

Mr. Darcy closed his eyes. "I was afraid of that. Reports have gotten back to me about him. However, I have promised Wickham, and I must keep my word as a gentleman."

Darcy frowned. "Yes, sir."

"Do you think he will accept it?"

Darcy shrugged. "I cannot think he will. George Wickham's main occupation is obtaining easy money. He would rather make his fortune by gambling than by working, or so it seems.”

They both were quiet for a long moment, Darcy looking at his hands while he waited for his father’s response. When it did not come, he looked up, expecting Mr. Darcy to have fallen asleep. Instead, it appeared his father was thinking.

“If he refuses it, offer him some money in its place. Two or three thousand ought to be plenty. I will consider my promise kept, in that case.” Mr. Darcy closed his eyes. “I am very tired, my son.”

“Sleep, then, and I will return when you awaken.” Darcy left the room then, pleased with his father’s solution to the problem of his steward’s son.

~~~***~~~

A couple weeks after his arrival at Pemberley, Darcy had opportunity to speak in depth to his father about Elizabeth.

“Are you well, Son? You seem distracted today.” Mr. Darcy reached out a hand and patted the younger man on the knee.

“I am well. I just-” He sighed. “I have been thinking about Elizabeth – Miss Elizabeth. I miss her.”

Mr. Darcy lifted one side of his lips. “You should write to her father. Perhaps he will reply and you will learn how she is doing.”
~~~

"I did write to him when I first arrived, but I have not heard back. I do not really expect to. We have had one or two brief conversations, but he is a rather indolent gentleman. Miss Elizabeth tells me he puts off correspondence as long as possible and is just as likely to not reply at all as he is to reply at the last possible moment."

"I see. I am sorry to hear this. From what you have told me of her, Miss Elizabeth is a lovely young woman."

That was all it took for Darcy to begin to wax eloquent about her, telling his father as many stories as he could recall about his time with the beautiful girl.

"Aunt Theodosia and Andrew do not approve of her."

Mr. Darcy's brow lifted. "It is none of their concern. I wrote to Joseph just after I got your letter and informed him of my approval. Now that I have heard from your own lips what she is like and how much you love her, I will tell you now: you have my permission to marry her. Do not let Theodosia or heaven forbid, Lady Catherine de Bourgh, to persuade you otherwise."

"Thank you, Father." Darcy lowered his head, playing with the corner of the folded-down blanket that lay on his father's bed. "What if she does not wait for me? I have nightmares about that. We are so far from each other and are not allowed to write. What if someone else comes along?"

"Son."

Darcy looked up.

"Based on your description, I do not think that will happen. If it should, then it was simply not meant to be and you will move on."

Darcy's heart protested his father's words, but he said nothing, instead nodding his acknowledgement.

~~~***~~~

Darcy's talks with his father after this one became increasingly shorter as the older man's health declined. He and Georgiana often spent entire days sitting in the master's chambers, talking to him, though he began to be more unresponsive than not. Five weeks and three days after Darcy arrived at Pemberley, his father passed away, his hands held by his children.

Now, the pain and longing in Darcy's heart for Elizabeth was joined by grief. The days and weeks of the next few months passed achingly slowly.
~~~

Chapter 10

Longbourn

Christmas Eve, 1805

Elizabeth looked up as her aunt approached the window seat where she was currently located. She moved her feet to give the other woman room to join her.

"Are you well, Lizzy? You have not been your usual cheerful self. Your father makes jokes about you being crossed in love, and Jane does her best to make you seem happy, but I can clearly see you are not. Do you wish to tell me about it?"

Elizabeth grimaced. "There is not much to tell. My father is probably correct."

Maddie took her niece's hand. "Were you crossed in love, then?"

"I do not know. Perhaps." Elizabeth looked down at her hand joined with her aunt's. "He was very attentive. He asked to call on me here, after the house party at Netherfield last August, and he did for a week or two. Then, he suddenly vanished. Mrs. Darcy told me he had been called home because his father was ill."

"And he never came back?"

"No, but … I heard, also from his aunt, that his father died. This was back in October, just after Michaelmas, so he is in mourning." Elizabeth sighed, her eyes filling with tears at the thought of Darcy's pain. "I understand why he left. What has me upset is what Mrs. Darcy said the day she told me he had been called home. She said they expect great things of him and that he is destined to marry well, and that she was certain I understood. But, when he spoke to me, he said things that made me sure he wished to marry me when his tour was over."

Maddie bit her lip. "I do not know what to say. She may be correct, or she may not. It is likely that his relatives do expect him to marry high. The Darcys of Pemberley are among the wealthiest families in all England. On the other hand, they are not known for being overly high in the instep. Mrs. Darcy is his aunt and not his mother; it is entirely possible what she thinks is not what his parents believe. Look at myself and your mother. Can there be two totally different points of view?"

Elizabeth chuckled through her tears. "No, I do not suppose there can be. Do you think there is reason to hope?"

Maddie shrugged. "I do not know. There may be, and there may not be. If he could write to you, it would be possible because he could explain himself, but he cannot, since you are not engaged."

Elizabeth looked down again. "True."

"Your uncle is asking your father for permission for you and Jane to come with us when we return to London. It will be good for you to have a change of scenery, I think. What do you say? Would you like to visit us for a while?"

"I would." A grateful smile spread over Elizabeth's face. "Thank you."

"Think nothing of it. We are delighted to be able to provide you girls this opportunity to see more of the world." Maddie let go of her niece's hand and changed the subject.

~~~***~~~

A fortnight later found Elizabeth and Jane in their uncle's carriage, along with Mr. Gardiner and his family, pulling up to his large home on Gracechurch Street, near Cheapside. Maddie's talk with Elizabeth had greatly cheered the girl, and while she was still heartbroken to be separated from Darcy and fearful that it would be permanent, she was better able to put on a good face for those around her. The Gardiners' children helped a great deal. It was difficult to be sad and fearful in the face of their unrelenting cheer.

It took a day or two for everyone to settle in, but soon, plans were being made for outings. Mr. Gardiner brought home a paper the day after they arrived and the four of them scanned it for events they might attend.
~~~

"It seems the museum has a special display of artifacts from Egypt through the end of the month. The article says it contains items not previously seen by the public." Gardiner folded the corner of the page down and looked over it at Elizabeth. "I know at least one of you will be eager to see that."

The ladies laughed.

"We all will, but I suspect Lizzy will be the most fascinated." Jane nudged her sister. "Is that not correct?"

Elizabeth blushed but laughed. "It is correct, yes."

Maddie turned to her husband. "What else is in there?"

Gardiner, his shoulders still shaking, pulled the newssheet back up. "There are lectures every Tuesday sponsored by the London Society for the Advancement of Science Studies. There are also some on Thursdays whose focus is modern literature." He pulled the paper closer to his face for a moment, then lowered it. "These alternate with lectures on older literature ... ancient texts, it says. All are held in public buildings and should be acceptable for gently-bred ladies to attend."

"Good," Maddie said. "Of course, you will accompany us, anyway."

Gardiner's brows lifted. "Of course!"

Maddie shook her head and rolled her eyes. "We also have invitations for dinners and balls. There was an entire stack of them waiting for us when we arrived the other day."

"I love balls." Elizabeth sighed, thinking of the one at Netherfield, and the handsome and attentive gentleman she could not stop thinking about and longing for.

"As do I." Jane looked at her aunt. "Will the gowns we brought be enough?"

"Oh no." Maddie shook her head. "Not at all. I have already sent a note around to my modiste, asking for an appointment. She is not the most fashionable of seamstresses, but she is excellent, and I have used her services for years."

"Lovely." It was Elizabeth's turn to roll her eyes. "Hours of standing around in one's chemise, being measured, pinned, poked, and prodded. What fun."

Jane, Maddie, and Gardiner laughed. Elizabeth's dislike of time spent at the modiste was well-known in the family.

"I promise not to abandon you, dear sister. You will not go through it alone." Jane patted Elizabeth's arm. Her words provoked more laughter.

~~~***~~~

A week later, Elizabeth and her relatives descended from their carriage in front of the building that housed the London Society for the Advancement of Science Studies. To-
~~~

night's lecture was about the geological formations of England, a topic that all four of them found fascinating.

They joined the small crowd entering the building and, upon finding the room in which the lecture was to be held, chose their seats. Elizabeth, especially, had a habit of watching people, and she and her sister were thus engaged when she noticed a tall gentleman wearing a black armband enter the room. Her breath caught. *It is him!* She shot to her feet, willing Darcy to look her way. She stared, unable to move her gaze from his handsome form.

Elizabeth knew the moment he saw her. He stopped dead in his tracks and stared, a delighted smile slowly spreading over his countenance. Though he had appeared to be choosing a seat closer to the door, he immediately walked down the row and across the aisle and almost before she knew it, stood before her. She looked up at him, her heart in her eyes.

"Miss Elizabeth." Darcy bowed. "I am beyond happy to see you again."

Elizabeth remembered to curtsey, but her mouth had gone dry. She swallowed once, and then greeted him with what sounded to her like a croak. "And I, you." She could say nothing more.

"Will you introduce me to your friends?" His deep, soothing voice did as it always had done, raising goose pimples all over her while at the same time easing her nerves.

"Yes, I will." She gestured to her right. "My sister you know."

Darcy bowed. "Indeed. Good evening, Miss Bennet."

Jane curtseyed and murmured a reply.

"This is my uncle, Mr. Edward Gardiner, and my aunt, Mrs. Gardiner."

Darcy bowed. "Edward Gardiner, the gun maker?"

Gardiner grinned and bowed again. "At your service. But do not tell anyone." He put a finger to his lips as he winked.

Darcy's lips twitched. "I will not. I must tell you that I admire your work, though."

"I thank you." Gardiner paused. "How do you know our Lizzy?"

"We met in Hertfordshire, at a house party my aunt and uncle held." Darcy turned his gaze from Gardiner to Elizabeth, and she could feel the tingle from her head to her toes.

"Will you sit with us, Mr. Darcy?" Maddie looked down the row of seats. "There is plenty of room."

"I will; thank you." Darcy tore his eyes from Elizabeth's and looked around. "I am meeting a friend here. There he is." He raised a hand and waved to a slightly shorter, thinner, red-haired gentleman, who immediately hastened across the room. "This is Mr. Charles Bingley. Do you mind if he joins us?"

"Not at all! The more the merrier." Gardiner waited for Darcy to introduce them all to his friend before moving out of the way. "I assume you will want to sit beside Lizzy."

"Yes, sir. Thank you for your tolerance." Darcy shoved Bingley down the row and took the seat Jane had been in, to Elizabeth's right.

Elizabeth clasped her hands tightly in her lap. She did not know what to make of Darcy's staring, or his agreement to sit with them and then to choose the seat right beside her.

"I cannot begin to express how pleased I am to see you, Miss Elizabeth." Darcy leaned down to whisper to her. When her eyes rose again to his, he continued. "I have missed you more than I can say."

She could not help herself at that point. All the longing for him she had suffered through rose up within her. "I have missed you, as well."

The lecture began then, and their opportunity for more conversation vanished. They sat beside each other in silence. Elizabeth heard the words being said, but her mind was on the gentleman at her side. She closed her eyes and silently prayed that he would renew his attentions to her, and that his aunt had been wrong about his family's expectations. All her hopes seemed to be answered when, at the end of the lecture and they all stood to leave, Darcy asked her a question.

"May I call on you tomorrow?"

Her heart pounding in her ears, Elizabeth nodded. "Yes. Oh, yes, please do."

Darcy smiled at her, and she thought she detected relief in his eyes. She listened as he asked permission from her uncle and obtained the address to their residence. Her pulse thundered as he offered to escort her to the carriage. She nodded and tucked her small hand into the crook of his elbow. When she felt the same tingle she always had, a bright smile lit up her face. So focused was she on her own feelings and experiences that she never noticed her sister's fascination with Darcy's friend.

Outside the lecture hall, Mr. Gardiner handed Maddie into the carriage then stepped back. Darcy and Elizabeth approached, turning to face each other. Darcy took her hand.

"Thank you for granting me permission to call on you. I look forward to our visit tomorrow." Darcy's eyes caressed Elizabeth's face as he lifted her hand and kissed it. Then, he assisted her into the equipage, his movements slow and, it seemed to her, lingering. She sat in her customary spot as he moved out of the way, and watched him through the window, delighted to see him watching her, as well. They remained in those positions, staring intently at each other, until the carriage moved away and they could see each other no more.

"Well, I never thought I would see the day that my eldest and most accomplished nieces would both, on the same evening, wear besotted looks upon their faces." Gardiner laughed when Elizabeth looked at him in surprise, then at Jane, who had turned to look at her with an identical expression.

Maddie joined him in teasing the girls. "I never did, either. And yet, the proof is before us."

Elizabeth blushed and shook her head. "What do you mean?"

"Why, you and Mr. Darcy, of course, and Jane and Mr. Bingley." Maddie laughed again when the younger girl's head swung back towards her sister. "Did you not notice?"

"No, I did not. Did you like him, Jane?"

"Very much. He was everything a young man ought to be: amiable, good-looking ..."

"And rich." The girls looked at their uncle. The sun was setting and the interior of the carriage was getting darker by the minute, but they could see the satisfied look on his face. "I am acquainted with his father. Carriage maker, originally from Scarborough. The rest of the family is in cotton, I believe, but he wanted to set out on his own. Make a name for himself, without the favors of his relatives. Word has it, he worked himself into an early grave, but died a wealthy man."

"There you go, Jane. He is therefore perfect and you may like him as much as you choose." Maddie nudged Jane's knee with her own.

"Aunt." Jane's protest was weak, and even Elizabeth giggled at it.

"Maybe he will visit along with Mr. Darcy. What do you think, Husband?"

"I do not know. He seemed to be just as taken with Jane as she was with him, but he did not ask permission to call. I suppose we will have to wait and see."

"You will not turn him away, will you?" There was a note in Jane's voice that was akin to panic.

"No." Gardiner chuckled. "I will not. My sister would have my head to turn a rich suitor away from you. If he comes with Darcy tomorrow, he will be welcomed."

"And, if he doesn't?" Though Maddie could not be seen at this point, Elizabeth knew from her tone of voice that her right brow had lifted.

"If he does not, I will have my investigator track him down and I will pay him a visit to let him know he is welcome."

"Uncle! Do not force him to call. I do not want a gentleman who must be pushed to attend me."

Another round of laughter filled the carriage. As it came to a stop in front of the Gardiner home, Maddie assured Jane he would not. "He is teasing you. I am quite certain Mr. Bingley will arrive with Mr. Darcy tomorrow. Mark my words."

<div style="text-align:center">~~~***~~~</div>

Mrs. Gardiner was correct. When Mr. Darcy knocked on the door precisely at one o'clock, Mr. Bingley was at his side. Elizabeth had not paid much attention to the other man last night, but as he was announced, she looked him over, delighted to see an expression on his face that matched her sister's.

Elizabeth smiled at Darcy as he approached and bowed to her.

Darcy accepted her unspoken offer of a seat beside her on the settee. "Should I be jealous of my friend?"

Elizabeth's brows shot up and she whipped around to face him. "Not at all. Why would you say that?"

Darcy tilted his head toward the sofa on the other side of the room. "You watched Bingley quite intently when he entered."

"Oh! No, it is just that I paid him no mind last night and my sister was quite taken with him. I wished to see what all the fuss was about, is all." Elizabeth blushed. She was happy beyond anything that Darcy was sitting next to her, but after the heartache of the last months, after being ignored for all that time, and after listening to Theodosia's voice repeating her expectations over and over in her head, she felt a reticence toward him she had never experienced before.

"Good." Darcy paused. "I would hate to have to call him out. I quite like him and would not be happy to lose such a steady friend."

Elizabeth nodded, biting her lip and looking at her hands, which were twisting together in her lap.

"Miss Elizabeth?"

She looked up.

"Are you well?"

She chewed her lip for a long moment, silently debating if she should ask him anything or simply wait and see what happened. Finally, though, she decided she would rather know ahead of time if he were only playing with her.

"Why did you not let me know you were leaving Hertfordshire?"

Darcy started. "What do you mean?"

Elizabeth's voice rose along with her hands. "I had no idea you were gone until the next evening."

"I wrote you a letter. Did Andrew not have it delivered?"

Elizabeth could feel her eyes widen at his words. She fell silent for a moment as she considered the implications of what he was saying. Then, she shook her head. "No, Mr. Darcy. I got no letter. Mr. Andrew Darcy did not come to Longbourn, and none of the Netherfield servants did. I asked your aunt the following evening, when we all dined at Lucas

Lodge, if you were well, and she told me you were called home to Pemberley."

Darcy looked her in the eye, his mien somber. "Andrew did not bring a letter to Longbourn, or have a servant do it for him?"

"No." Elizabeth shook her head. "He did not. I know because I watched at the window all morning, and after our walk to Meryton, I checked with Mrs. Hill. She said no one had been there at all." As she finished speaking, Elizabeth could see Darcy's jaw tense.

"Why, that dirty, rotten-" Darcy stopped speaking. He swallowed and took a breath. "I am so sorry, Miss Elizabeth. I did write you a letter. I handed it to Andrew with strict instructions to have it delivered to you and that he was to send a servant with it if he did not wish to take it himself. I *told* him that my father approved of you and that I expected him to do as I asked, because we are cousins and family takes care of family. Please, forgive me."

Chapter 11

Darcy reminded himself to remain calm as he awaited Elizabeth's response. His anger with his cousin was great, but now was not the time to think about it. *I will deal with Andrew later,* he thought. *I know they are in town for the season, and it will be weeks before Aunt Theodosia goes back to Hertfordshire while Uncle Joseph goes out on the circuit. I have plenty of time.*

"I do forgive you. You did what you could to notify me. It was up to others to follow through. It is not your fault they did not do as you asked."

Darcy breathed a sigh of relief. "Thank you. You are everything gracious and kind."

Elizabeth smiled but said nothing else.

"I hesitate to ask, because I suspect I know what your reply will be, but ... I wrote to your father the day I arrived at Pemberley and had my man post it. I asked Mr. Bennet to let you know I had made it home and to relay to you my regard." Darcy searched her face again, his heart falling when her brow creased.

"Papa never told me he received anything from you. He did, however, take a great deal of enjoyment from teasing me about being crossed in love." Elizabeth's eyes rolled.

Darcy closed his eyes as a new wave of anger filled him. When he opened them, he spoke carefully. "I am so sorry." He shook his head. "That I chose two different messengers and neither of them did as I asked fills me with dismay. I am surprised that you agreed to accept my call, under the circumstances."

Elizabeth was quiet for a long moment, then, glancing toward her relatives, laid her hand on his arm for a brief second, just long enough to release an arrow of feeling up to his heart.

"I cannot fault you in the matter. My father is a dilatory correspondent, at best. I hate to sound like Jane, but it is possible that your letter was carelessly tossed into a drawer to be read later and then forgotten about. It has happened before. I cannot be angry at you for his lapse any more than I can for that of your cousin."

Darcy reached over and took the hand that was closest to his, lifting it to his lips and kissing the fingers. "You are too kind, Miss Elizabeth." He reluctantly released her hand, lowering it slowly. "As you see, I am still in mourning, so I must be circumspect, but I should like to call on you again. How long will you be in town?"

"We will be here until the end of February, at least. Papa has given permission for a visit of eight weeks." Elizabeth blushed and looked down. Her next words were so softly spoken that

Darcy had to lean his head down to hear them. "I should very much like you to call again."

Maddie drew the couple's attention. "Mr. Darcy, I was just telling Mr. Bingley that we intend to visit the British Museum this coming Saturday. I have invited him to accompany us, and now invite you to come along, as well. A museum visit is not out of the question for one in mourning. Will you take the tour with us?"

Darcy's lips lifted in a smile. "I would love to. I have always enjoyed seeing the collection there."

"Excellent." Maddie clapped her hands. "Would you like to meet us there? You are closer; it might make more sense for you to arrive separately, rather than for you to come all the way here and ride all the way back with us."

Darcy thought about it for a minute and then nodded. "I would not at all mind making the trip to your home, but given my mourning, I have added incentive to do as you suggest. What time shall we meet?"

"I will have to consult with my husband to confirm, but will one o'clock be acceptable?"

"It sounds very good to me." Darcy turned his gaze toward his friend. "What say you, Bingley?"

Bingley jumped a little, as though surprised to be addressed. He looked away from Jane and made his reply. "I agree."

Darcy laughed. "What does that mean? I think you were not paying attention and have no idea what you just agreed to."

Bingley's countenance soon matched his hair. He was clearly embarrassed, but he jovially replied. "I confess I was not. What did you need to know?"

Darcy shook his head but refrained from teasing his friend any further. "Will you be able to join me in a visit to the British Museum at one o'clock on Saturday? We will be meeting Mrs. Gardiner and her husband and nieces there."

"Of course, I will." Bingley smiled brightly. "I will arrive at Darcy House at thirty minutes before the hour, ready to board your coach and ride along."

"Excellent!" Maddie chuckled. "We will look forward to seeing you both there."

Darcy glanced at the clock. He did not wish to leave, but they had stayed well beyond the quarter hour that was usually acceptable for a call. Sighing internally, he stood. "We should be going." He bowed to Elizabeth, who had risen when he did. "I apologize again for damaging your trust in my integrity, no matter how inadvertently or unknowingly it was done." He reached for her hand as he stared into her eyes. "I would like the opportunity to regain that trust. I thank you for your permission to call, and I look forward to escorting you around the museum on Saturday." He kissed her hand again before letting it go. Stepping back, he said, "It will be a long wait."

"It will." Elizabeth lifted her chin. "But, we have waited four long months to see each other, with no idea if we actually would or not. Perhaps the next couple of days will fly by."

"I hope they do." Darcy's words were soft. "Will you walk me out?"

"Yes, Lizzy, do walk Mr. Darcy to the door. Jane, will you do the same for Mr. Bingley?" Maddie curtseyed to the gentlemen. "Thank you for your visit. We look forward to seeing you again."

Both men bowed to their hostess, then offered their elbows to their respective ladies. The four of them waited in the entry hall while the maid got their coats and hats. They were quiet for the two or three minutes it took for the gentlemen to don their outerwear.

Darcy did not mind the silence. His heart was too full at the moment to be talkative. He was overjoyed to be standing in front of his heart's desire after so many months without her. At the same time, he was too angry with his cousin and her father to be able to truly give Elizabeth the attention he wished to. Finally, the moment came when he had to depart. He bowed deeply to her.

"Until Saturday, Miss Elizabeth. Do not forget me."

Elizabeth's curtsey matched his bow for depth. "I could never forget you." She smiled warmly at him.

Darcy's heart lifted. He said nothing else, instead opening the door and departing.

~~~***~~~

Late Saturday morning, Darcy was unsettled. He had spent the last three nights barely sleeping, angry at Andrew and Mr. Bennet and worried that he would be unable to earn Elizabeth's hand because of their interference. His cousin earned the better part of his ire, because Andrew had been given explicit instructions and a reminder that family does for family. Darcy's father had continually expounded on that concept while he was growing up. Family was everything to the Darcys. *Except, it seems, in Andrew's case,* he thought sourly.

He breathed in deeply through his nose as he stared into the pier glass, and then exhaled the same way. "I must control my feelings." He was breaking his fast with his sister, a habit he had begun after the death of their father. "Georgiana does not need to see my anger. She should be surrounded with love at this time." Tugging on the bottom of his waistcoat, he took one more deep breath and turned away, striding to the door and out into the hallway.
~~~

A few minutes later, Darcy entered the breakfast nook off the dining room. Georgiana was not yet downstairs, so he requested coffee of the footman on duty and set about preparing a plate for himself. He no more than seated himself when his sister appeared in the doorway.

"Good morning, Brother." Georgiana skipped across the room to Darcy's side, throwing her arms around him for a hug.

"Good morning, Sister." Darcy held her close for a long minute, then kissed her head and let go. "What would you like to eat this morning?" He gestured to the footman, who stepped to the sideboard and picked up a plate.

"I do not know just yet." Georgiana whirled around and hurried to the side of the room. She spent a few minutes on tiptoes, looking at the items on offer and directing the servant as to which she wanted to eat. Darcy sipped his coffee as he watched her charm the man into smiling as he assisted her.

When she had made her selections, Georgiana returned to the table and plopped down into the chair to Darcy's right.

Darcy nodded his thanks to the servant.

"Shall we say grace before we eat? Miss Fitzhugh always says grace." Georgiana rested her wrists on the edge of the table, her fingers intertwined, and bowed her head.

"Of course, we shall." Darcy bowed his own head and recited a simple prayer, then lifted his fork. "How do you like Miss Fitzhugh?"

"I like her very much!" Georgiana carefully cut her ham into pieces as she spoke. "She makes my lessons seem interesting, even the boring subjects."

Darcy chuckled. "Which are the boring ones?"

"History, mainly. Sometimes reading. I like to read when the stories are interesting, but sometimes I must read things that I do not like, and that makes it boring."

Darcy's lips twitched. "I see. Are reading or history on your schedule of lessons for the day?"

"Oh, we read every day, but thankfully, there will be no history today. I have a music lesson. On the pianoforte." Georgiana stabbed a piece of meat with her fork.

"As I recall, you enjoy the pianoforte."

"Yes, excessively." With a firm nod, she shoved the forkful of ham into her mouth and began to chew.

Darcy chuckled again. He took a few bites of his own meal, thinking how delightful it was to spend time with his sister. He looked at the place on his other side. *The only thing that would make it better would be for Eliza-beth to be here.* He sighed to himself.

"What do you have to do today, Fitzwilliam?"

Darcy swallowed, sipped his coffee, and then made his reply. "I am meeting Bingley and some friends at the museum this afternoon."

"That sounds like fun. Miss Fitzhugh has described to me some of the exhibits. When I get older, I should like to see them for myself." She forked more food into her mouth. Before she was done swallowing, she asked a question.

Darcy smirked. "I am sorry, Pest, I could not understand you. Swallow, then try again."

Georgiana blushed but obeyed. "Are Mr. Bingley's sisters going along today?"

"No, I believe Miss Bingley is preparing for her wedding and Miss Caroline is still in school. Bingley will not retrieve her until the day before the ceremony, which is still several days away." He paused to sip his coffee. "Do you remember me speaking of Miss Elizabeth Bennet when we were at Pemberley?"

Georgiana sat up straight, turning eager eyes toward her brother. "I do. Is she in London? Is that whom you will be at the museum with?"

Darcy nodded, a soft smile lifting his lips. "I saw her on Tuesday at that lecture I attended. You remember, I told you about it?" When his sister nodded, he continued. "She was there, and she gave me permission to call on her, which I did on Wednesday. She is staying with her aunt and uncle, the Gardiners, and it was Mrs. Gardiner who suggested I attend them on the tour." He shrugged. "I could not say no."

"Did Mr. Bingley go to their house with you?"

"He did. I think he likes Miss Elizabeth's sister." Darcy leaned down close to his sister's ear. "He paid no attention to anyone else and stared at her the entire time we were visiting." He grinned when Georgiana giggled.

After that exchange, the pair finished breaking their fasts and separated with another hug and a promise from Darcy to listen to her play in the evening.

Chapter 12

Elizabeth had not looked forward to anything in a long time as much as she had looked forward to this museum visit. She glanced across the seat to Jane, who sat as serenely as always but who watched out the window with a dreamy smile.

"Are you excited, Lizzy?" Maddie smirked at her younger niece, looking down at her hand where it rested on the seat.

Elizabeth suddenly realized she had been drumming her fingers and clenched them into a fist as she blushed. She lifted her chin. "I am. It has been a long time since I have spent much time with Mr. Darcy where we could talk. I have so much to say ..." She trailed off.

Maddie nodded sympathetically. "And now that you have found each other again, he is in mourning and cannot call as freely as he would like."

Elizabeth sighed. "Yes."

"Well, you will not have to wait much longer." Mr. Gardiner nodded his head toward the window. "He seems to be waiting for you."

Elizabeth sat straight up as the carriage came to a stop. She waited impatiently as her uncle disembarked and handed out her aunt and sister. When her turn came, a hand connected to an arm in a different color of cloth than her uncle was wearing was extended toward her. She slowly reached her own hand toward the gloved one waiting for her at the same time that her eyes lifted to take in the gentleman's identity. When she realized it was Darcy, she inhaled sharply, then felt a grin lift her lips. She laid her palm in his and allowed him to assist her out of the equipage.

"Good afternoon, Miss Elizabeth." Darcy's deep voice did as it always had: it both warmed her and made her shiver in excitement.

"Good afternoon, Mr. Darcy." She noted that he had not let go of her hand and was instead tucking it into the crook of his elbow. She sighed happily. "Have you been waiting long?"

"No; we arrived just a few minutes ago. My carriage probably rounded the corner just as yours came to a stop." Darcy held her hand tightly to his side. "I am happy to see you again."

Elizabeth looked up at him, her eyes twinkling. She did not bother to hide her approbation, allowing her smile to convey her admiration. "My feelings match yours exactly."

Gardiner's chuckle penetrated their bubble. "Shall we go inside?" He gestured to the steps leading into the building.

Darcy led Elizabeth in, the Gardiners following, with Bingley and Jane coming behind them. Darcy paid the admission fee for the entire group, over the protests of his friends. "Perhaps we can go to Gunter's afterwards, and you can buy us ices," he suggested to Gardiner.

Maddie's eyes widened. She turned eagerly to her husband. "Oh, Gunter's! Yes, dear … do say you will."

Gardiner shook his head. "You, sir, have just hit upon my wife's favorite thing in all of London." He laughed. "Very well. You get us in here, and I will provide ices."

Darcy laughed. "Good. Shall we proceed?"

The group spent a delightful couple of hours, viewing the exhibits and discussing them, followed by the promised treat.

"You must come to dine with us one evening." Maddie extended the invitation to both gentlemen. "Perhaps Tuesday? We will keep the guest list to just the pair of you."

Bingley shook his head, looking sadly at Jane. "I am afraid I will not be able to attend. That is the day before my younger sister's wedding, and I must retrieve my youngest sister from her school so she can stand up with Louisa."

"That is completely understandable," Jane said, her serene smile giving no indication of how she really felt about it.

"I will be happy to come." Darcy thanked Maddie for the invitation.

"We will be happy to have you." Maddie turned to Bingley. "Perhaps you will be able to come another day, Mr. Bingley?"

Bingley's countenance immediately brightened. "I could, yes! Once I get my youngest sister back to her school and my oldest off on her wedding trip, I will be free to visit as often as I wish to." He blushed. "Or, at least, as often as you and Miss Bennet will allow."

Maddie smiled. "You may come as often as you wish; I am certain Jane would be happy to entertain you whenever you visit."

It was now Jane's turn to blush. She looked down, making her next words almost too soft to hear. "Indeed, I would."

After a few more words of assurance, the party split up, the Gardiners taking their nieces home to Gracechurch Street and Darcy departing with Bingley.

~~~***~~~

The following Tuesday evening, Darcy arrived earlier than required. Elizabeth was sitting in the window seat in the drawing room and spied his carriage pulling up. Though the light was dim, as the sun had set and the lanterns on the house and wrought iron gate only illuminated the area so much, she could tell it was her suitor because of the size of the equipage. Her uncle's was older and smaller.

When Elizabeth saw Darcy's tall form step down, her heart skipped a beat. She stood, a smile spreading over her face, and spun away from the window and toward her gathered family. "He is here!" Suddenly nervous, she
~~~

smoothed her hands over her skirt and touched her hair.

"You look well, Lizzy." Jane moved to stand near her sister, reaching out a hand to squeeze Elizabeth's. "I daresay he would never notice if you did not."

Elizabeth giggled. "Thank you." Impulsively, she turned and threw her arms around Jane, hugging her tightly.

Jane hugged her in return, quickly but firmly, then let go and stepped back.

The door opened and the maid stepped in to announce the visitor. "Mr. Darcy." She curtseyed and then stepped out of the way, to be replaced by the gentleman.

"Welcome, Mr. Darcy." Maddie graciously welcomed their guest. "We are happy to see you again."

Darcy bowed. Elizabeth noticed that his gaze was riveted upon her already.

"Thank you, ma'am. I am happy to be here."

Maddie gestured toward her younger niece. "Why do you not sit beside Elizabeth? Jane and I will take the chairs. We are waiting for Mr. Gardiner to come home from his warehouse, and he will be a little bit, so we have time to visit."

With a nod and a murmured, "Thank you," Darcy did as she suggested.

Elizabeth smiled at him again and made a show of moving over to leave him room on the sofa beside her. She curtseyed to him when he bowed before her and took her hand. "Good evening, sir."

Darcy kissed her fingers. "Good evening. I am delighted to be in your presence once more."

Elizabeth replied by broadening her smile. She gestured to the furniture behind them and sat down upon it. Darcy followed suit, and soon, the two of them were conversing as though they had not been separated by days or even weeks.

Once Gardiner arrived and had washed up and changed his clothes, the group gathered in the dining room.

Maddie nodded toward the table. "Sit where ever you like, Mr. Darcy. We do not stand on formality when the children do not join us."

Darcy's brows rose for a second. "They are not dining with us tonight?"

Maddie shook her head. "No. They had a long day yesterday and as a result, their behavior today did not warrant such a treat. Perhaps the next time you visit, they can come down to greet you, but tonight, it is supper in the nursery and an early bedtime."

As soon as everyone was settled into a seat at the small table, the maid, cook, and footman began to bring dishes out and serve. Conversation was kept to general topics like the weather. Once the servants had been dismissed, it became more lively and covered a variety of topics. Eventually, though, the food was consumed and the ladies retired to the drawing room. Elizabeth waited impatiently for the gentlemen to join her and her sister and aunt.

"Do sit down, Lizzy." Maddie's exclamation startled her younger niece out of her thoughts. "Pacing back and forth now will not bring Mr. Darcy here any faster than watching for him in the window did earlier."

Elizabeth felt herself flush as she obeyed. "Jane said the same to me at Longbourn once."

Jane smirked. "I did, and yet, you are still pacing."

Elizabeth rolled her eyes but ignored her sister. "What were we talking about?" She did her best to participate in the discussion while still trying to listen for the footsteps of the gentlemen.

Eventually, her wishes were answered, and her uncle opened the drawing room door and gestured Darcy in ahead of him. Elizabeth, Jane, and Maddie rose from their seats.

With a rush of relief, Elizabeth felt some of the tension in her body release. She smiled brightly at Darcy.

"Well, ladies," Gardiner teased, "what have you been up to while we were not among you?"

Everyone laughed, as Elizabeth suspected her uncle had intended they would.

Maddie's hands landed on her hips. "I am sure you would like to know, but none of us intend to tell you." She tossed her head and sniffed, causing more laughter.

"I am sure I can get it out of you later, Wife, so I will let it go for now." Gardiner winked at Maddie and then turned to his guest. "Please sit. I am certain my niece has been saving that spot on the sofa for you."

Darcy grinned and inclined his head. "Thank you. I think I will."

Elizabeth's smile remained bright as her suitor approached and then bowed before her. She curtseyed in response, and then seated herself, waving her hand over the seat beside her. "We have much to discuss, sir." She glanced to where her aunt and uncle sat a few feet away. "I hope we will not be disturbed before we get through it all." She looked back at Darcy, who nodded.

"We do," he said. "Let me begin by apologizing once more that my cousin did not deliver my note to you, and that the information in my letter to your father did not reach you, either. The very thing that I wished to avoid is, I fear, exactly what happened, and you thought I had abandoned you." A crease appeared between Darcy's brows as he spoke.

Elizabeth nodded, her own forehead furrowing. "I did, it is true, but it was not only the lack of correspondence that led me to believe you had."

Darcy tilted his head. "What do you mean?" He sounded perplexed.

Elizabeth took a deep breath and looked down at her hands, which she held in her lap, tightly clasped. "It was Mrs. Darcy who told me that you had been called home and that your father was ill. She-" She fell silent.

"She what, Miss Elizabeth?" Darcy asked the question in a voice so soft he could barely be heard.

Elizabeth swallowed hard, then inhaled deeply and straightened her shoulders. She lifted her chin, looking him directly in the eyes. "She made it plain that you are expected to make an excellent marriage, and that it would never be to me." She paused. "She did not use those words, but the implication was clear." Even as she told the story, she could hear Theodosia's words ringing in her head. *He is destined for great things, including making a spectacular marriage. We have high hopes for him.* She mentally admonished herself and forced her attention back to the conversation at hand.

Darcy shook his head. Elizabeth could see that his jaw was clenched.

"My aunt should not have said that to you." He stared into her eyes, and Elizabeth felt as though he were trying to inject his words directly into her soul. "Her opinions are not those of the entirety of my family. My father gave me written permission to court you after I sent him a letter telling him everything I knew about you. He never stood for judging a person based on their social class. He told me himself that he had written to my uncle, telling him of his consent to my courting you.

"I discovered on that trip to Netherfield that my aunt clearly did not share that opinion. Neither did Andrew, though Grace seemed to be far more accepting. My uncle never shared his thoughts with me, so I do not know how he feels now or did then. When I gave my missive to you to my cousin, I reminded him that family does for family without regard to personal feelings. Apparently, he does not subscribe to that motto. I have not seen him or my aunt and uncle as of yet, but I assure you that when I do, I intend to take him to task for it."

Elizabeth bit her lip. "So, you are saying your family approves of you courting me?"

"My father did, and that is all the approval I need, other than yours."

Elizabeth closed her eyes as her shoulders sagged slightly for a brief moment. She straightened again as Darcy continued to speak.

"The judge was my father's only brother. He had three sisters, all of whom are married with families. They are spread out all over the country and I rarely see them. However, they have never behaved as Theodosia did, that I am aware of. They have been very welcoming to my friend Bingley when he and I have visited them these last four years.

"On my mother's side, I am more uncertain of your reception. Well, at least as far as my aunt goes. Lady Catherine de Bourgh is my mother's younger sister. She has always fancied the thought of me marrying her only surviving child, a girl named Anne. My father explained to me that, no matter what my aunt says my mother agreed to, I am under no obligation to marry my cousin. I have no intentions of doing so, no matter what happens." He paused, again staring intently into Elizabeth's eyes.

Chapter 13

Darcy waited until Elizabeth slowly nodded before he continued. "That particular aunt will be unhappy with a courtship between us. And I do intend to court you when my mourning is over, if you will allow it."

He watched as a blush stole over his companion's features. "I would allow it. I should very much like it."

Darcy's chest filled with happiness at Elizabeth's words. "Thank you." He wished he could hold her hand, but that would have been unacceptable even if they were engaged. He contented himself with merely gazing at her.

"Did your mother have any other siblings?"

Darcy started. He had forgotten what they were talking about. "Yes, she has a brother. He is an earl, and his seat is Matlock."

Elizabeth nodded, biting her lip again. Darcy forced his gaze away from her mouth to her eyes.

"It is hard to say what his reaction will be. On the one hand, he greatly admired my father and knew of his wishes and hopes for me. On the other hand, he would want me to marry to his political advantage, which I would not do had I never met you." Darcy shrugged, at a loss as to how to explain the situation fully.

"I do not know for certain that his desire for political gain will be outweighed by his duty to follow my father's wishes, but I suspect he will adhere to them. I hope he will, anyway." He thought for a moment. "As a matter of fact, I think I will visit him in the next few days and discover for myself. A few well-placed questions ought to do the trick."

He suddenly noticed Elizabeth's apprehensive look and immediately tried to ease her mind. "He is not unreasonable. Even if he were to object, if I stand firm, he will eventually see the uselessness of his arguments and give over. Do not fear. I promise you it will be well."

Darcy saw Elizabeth's shoulders lift and fall in a sigh.

"Very well," she said. "I will trust you in this. What of your other cousins? I assume the earl has at least one child?"

Darcy smiled. "He has four, two sons and two daughters. Viscount Tansley is courting a lovely young lady named Vanessa. She is the daughter of a marquis from Essex. After him comes Richard, who is a captain in the regulars and who declares he will never marry. He shares guardianship of my sister with me and we have been close friends since childhood. Their sisters are still at home. They are Lady Constance Fitzwilliam and Lady Susan Fitzwilliam. Tansley and Fitzwilliam will both be happy for me."

Elizabeth tilted her head. "Fitzwilliam?"

Darcy nodded. "Fitzwilliam is the family name."

Elizabeth's chin rose as understanding swept her features. "Oh, yes, that does make sense." She smiled. "I am happy to know you have at least some relatives who approve of your choices."

Darcy's smile returned. "My father and I spoke of you often. He wished to know everything about you and about my visits and our walks together. He expressed to me his joy that I had found someone to spend my life with. That was his goal in sending me to my uncle's house party, or so he said."

Elizabeth laughed, making Darcy's smile spread out into a grin.

The rest of the evening passed quickly in conversation between themselves, as well as with Jane and the Gardiners.

<div align="center">~~~***~~~</div>

The following day, Darcy was reviewing his correspondence when he noticed a letter in Theodosia's handwriting. He opened it to find an invitation to a family dinner. His aunt wrote that Andrew was in town for a fortnight to visit before he returned to University, and she wished for the family to get together once before he left.

Andrew and his perfidy were not far from Darcy's mind, and he swiftly wrote out a reply, accepting Theodosia's invitation. He placed the sealed note in the pile of outgoing mail. Then, glancing at his pocket watch and noting the time, cleaned up his desk and walked out of the room, heading up the stairs.

Darcy House was one of the older and larger homes in the Mayfair district. It was six stories tall, if one included the basement level, and was twice as wide and deep as most London houses. It boasted at least twice the number of bedrooms, as well as a large ballroom, a good-sized library, and two drawing rooms in the public area of the house. The top floor contained a small nursery with a schoolroom, along with rooms for the servants. The nursery was Darcy's destination.

Georgiana and her governess had come to London with him. He was to take tea with his sister today, in the schoolroom.

He entered the room just as Georgiana was putting her art supplies away.

"Good afternoon, my dear." Darcy strolled toward the ladies. "Miss Fitzhugh." He nodded to the governess and bowed shallowly.

"Good afternoon, Brother." Georgiana greeted Darcy with a happy smile.

"Good afternoon, sir." Miss Fitzhugh curtseyed. "If you will excuse me, I will fetch the tea things."

Darcy nodded, dismissing her to her work, then turned to his sister. "How was your art lesson?"

"We painted with watercolors." Georgiana took his hand and led him to an easel near the window, where a large piece of paper was clipped up to dry. "I cannot see anything but sky from the windows here, but I imagined being at Pemberley, in Mama's gardens."

Darcy tilted his head as he looked at the painting. "You did very well. I can see the iron bench you love so much around that tree." He pointed to an uneven splash of white at the base of a tall brown streak that was topped with green.

Georgiana grinned. "How did I do?"

"It is lovely," Darcy declared. "I can clearly make out the tree, the bench, and the flowers in the background. It is almost as though I am at home, looking at it with my own eyes. It is not perfect, but it is excellent. Good work, Sister!"

Georgiana beamed, and Darcy was happy he had praised her. His words had been truthful, but the painting was not perfect. He did not wish for her to be overly confident when she was only a beginner. However, he could not bear to disappoint her. Only praise and good things for his sister, who had lost so much in her decade of life.

The governess returned at that point, along with a maid who carried a tray of tea things. Both girls set their burdens down on the table in the center of the room, then Miss Fitzhugh began to prepare the tea as the maid returned to her chores. When the tea had steeped and her charge and employer had been served, Georgiana's cup containing mostly milk and very little actual tea, the governess curtseyed again and excused herself.

Darcy served his sister and himself some of the meats, cheeses, bread, and fruits that were on the trays. As they ate, they chatted together about Georgiana's lessons and Darcy's letters.

"There is someone I would like you to meet." Darcy set his cup down into its saucer as he watched his sister pop a piece of bread into her mouth and chew.

"Who?"

"Miss Elizabeth Bennet."

Georgiana brightened. "Have you seen her again?"

Darcy nodded. "I have. We have been in company three times now, and I have an invitation to dine there again in a few days. I would like to bring you with me, if you would like to go. The Gardiners' children often eat with them, to practice their manners. I am certain you would like them. They are very well-behaved but not in the least insipid or boring."

Georgiana tilted her head and watched her brother with a sharp expression. "Are they girls or boys?"

"One of each. Well, they have two younger children, as well, but they are babies and will remain in the nursery."

Georgiana gave one firm nod of her head, reminding her brother of their Aunt Catherine, which caused a shudder to roll up his spine.

"I will go with you. If they were both boys, I would decline, but I should very much like to have another girl to play with, even if it is only for an evening."

Darcy winced inside. One of his worries as her guardian had been that Georgiana would be lonely. *If they get along, I should encourage the relationship,* he thought. "Good," he said. "They are a couple years younger than you, but not so young that play would be impossible."

With a shrug, Georgiana picked up her last biscuit. "I do not mind. I look forward to meeting them, and Miss Bennet." She popped the treat in her mouth.

Darcy shook his head and chose not to rebuke her for stuffing an entire biscuit into her mouth at one time. Instead, he drained his cup and reached for his last piece of shortbread. "Would you like to walk for a minute around the garden?"

"Oh, yes, please!" She finished her tea and wiped her mouth with her napkin, then stood.

Darcy held his elbow out for Georgiana to take. He escorted her down to the gardens for a pleasant half-hour out in nature.

~~~***~~~

A couple days later, the evening of the family dinner at Judge Darcy's London home arrived. Darcy dropped in at the townhouse a little early, which he had indicated he would in his note of acceptance. He had spent many of the intervening days contemplating what he would say to his relatives, and how. As time passed, his anger at Andrew's actions grew instead of diminishing. Now, he stood behind his uncle's butler as the man announced him, gritting his teeth in an effort to maintain control of his temper.

"Mr. Fitzwilliam Darcy." The elderly servant bowed, gesturing the young man into the room.

Darcy entered with his spine erect and his hands clenched at his sides. He bowed and greeted his aunt, uncle, and cousins but said nothing else, at first.

"Do come in." Theodosia waved him closer. "Tell us how you have been managing. What have you done to keep yourself occupied? Have you met any young ladies?"

Darcy seated himself as his aunt had directed. Her final question gave him the opening he had been looking for, so he plunged in.

"I have not. I am in mourning for nine more months; I cannot socialize."

Theodosia interrupted. "That does not mean you cannot meet new people. Surely you have
~~~

been to a lecture or two, or visited the museums. Has your mother's family not introduced you to some beautiful heiress by now? You are a catch, you know, even more so than you were before your father passed."

"It does not matter that I am a catch, Aunt. My heart is taken and you know it." Darcy stood, unable to contain himself any longer. "Miss Elizabeth Bennet is everything lovely and it is she who has captured my attention."

Theodosia also rose to her feet. "She is beneath you! Have you been back to Hertfordshire? I thought for sure you would have forgotten all about her by now."

"I did not." Darcy forced the words out between his clenched teeth. He could feel his neck and shoulders tensing. "What were you thinking, telling her that she was not good enough for me? Who gave you the right to speak for me and, at the time, my father?"

The judge stepped between his wife and nephew. "Darcy."

"I am sorry, sir, but the words needed to be said."

Joseph nodded and then turned to his wife. "What is he speaking of, Theo? Surely you did not do what he accuses you of."

Darcy watched his aunt redden at her husband's words. "Well-" She stammered her reply. "Um-, well-, actually ..."

Joseph's jaw dropped and his eyes widened. "You did?" When Theodosia cast her gaze to the floor and nodded, he sighed and shook his head. "I told you what George said in his letter: that Fitzwilliam had written to him about Miss Elizabeth and he heartily approved of the match." His hands landed on his hips. "I thought you understood that you were to stay out of the matter. What possessed you to disobey me?"

Theodosia's lips thinned and she looked up at her husband, arms soon mimicking his pose. "George Darcy was not there to see that family. How are the Darcys to maintain their position in society if Fitzwilliam ties himself irrevocably to that awful family? They have ties to *trade*, for goodness' sake!"

"*I* have ties to trade, Madam, through *you!*" Joseph nearly roared his response, causing everyone in the room to jump. He turned to his nephew. "This is not all, is it?" He looked at his son, who was seated on the edge of a chair a few feet away and looking as though he wished to be anywhere else. "Of my two children, Grace holds more of my views than Andrew does. Did he take part in his mother's duplicity?"

"Actually, yes, sir, he did. I hold more anger toward him than to my aunt, for in my opinion, his sin is greater." Darcy turned from Joseph and Theodosia to his cousin. "I wrote a note to Elizabeth telling her that I had to leave but that

I would be back, though I did not know when. I gave it to Andrew and reminded him that Darcys take care of Darcys, regardless of our personal feelings about their actions. I was certainly raised that way, and I know my father was, for it was he who taught me."

"Indeed, your grandfather taught all of us that lesson. Family is family, and family takes care of family. I have taught my own children the same."

"Apparently not, sir, because Andrew never had the message delivered." Darcy's intense gaze drilled into his cousin's eyes. "I told him to send a servant if he did not wish to go himself. Miss Elizabeth told me that no message was received. She had expected one, because we had planned to walk into Meryton with her sisters. She interrogated Longbourn's staff, but they all denied a messenger from Netherfield making any delivery at all."

Andrew leaped to his feet. "How do you even know this? I did what I thought was correct. She *is* below you. Uncle George, if he did give you permission to court her, was wrong. Clearly, he was not in his right mind if he did not immediately call you home."

Before the young man could say anything else, Darcy took two long strides and was before him. He snatched his cousin up by the other man's cravat. "Do not dare disparage my father, *especially* to me." He felt his arm being pulled and realized his uncle was attempting to insert himself between them. He let go of the knot in Andrew's neck cloth and stepped back, but he remained stiff and angry, with his fists clenched at his sides. He was ready to pummel the younger man if he spoke out of line again.

As soon as Darcy stepped back, Joseph turned on his son. "That is enough, Andrew Marshall Darcy! What is the matter with you?" He ordered his wife and children to sit. "You, as well, Nephew, though I know you have inherited your father's need to move when distressed."

Darcy gave his uncle a single, tight nod. He chose a chair on the far side of the sofa from his cousin and perched on the edge.

"Tell us how you discovered these facts." Joseph held up a hand. "After your aunt tells the cook to hold our meal for a quarter hour."

Darcy used the few minutes Theodosia was out of the room to breathe deeply and remind himself that these were his family members, no matter how poorly some of them had treated him and the woman he loved.

"Very well, now," Joseph said as his wife returned to her seat. "Go ahead and tell us how you know what was said and not done."

"As you know, I arrived in London just over a fortnight ago. Two weeks ago tomorrow, I attended a lecture, and there, sitting on the far side of the hall, were Miss Bennet and Miss

Elizabeth, along with their aunt and uncle, with whom they are staying for a few weeks."

Theodosia sniffed. "The ones in *trade*? What were they doing at a lecture?"

"Wife, if you do not cease and desist this instant, I will suspend your pin money for the remainder of our time in town." Joseph's growled words made Theodosia's eyes widen and her lips thin. She lifted her chin and straightened her spine, clenching her jaw and looking for all the world like she never intended to speak again.

"Continue, Fitzwilliam, please. And do forgive your aunt." Joseph cast what appeared to Darcy to be a displeased eye toward his wife.

"Miss Elizabeth was not herself, at least not at first. I asked permission to call on her at her uncle's house the following day. I will not go into details except to say that I was given this information by the lady herself. Miss Bennet confirmed everything her sister said. I have no reason to believe other than that the ladies told the truth, for I saw evidence when we were all at Netherfield of my aunt's stiff-necked behavior toward the Bennets and others in the neighborhood. And, I knew Andrew agreed with her, which was why I was so firm in my request. I had hoped his loyalty to me would trump his biases. If I had known how wrong I was, I would have delayed my departure and gone to Longbourn to speak to her myself." Darcy glared again at Andrew.

"I am so sorry. On behalf of my wife and son, I apologize to you. Is Miss Elizabeth well?"

"She was very distrustful of me at first. Her hurt was deep when she thought I had abandoned her. We had some very painful conversations to get through for me to begin to rebuild her trust." Darcy paused. "I thank you for your apology, Uncle, but it would mean more if it came from your wife and son."

"I agree wholeheartedly." Joseph spun in his seat to face Theodosia and Andrew. "I expect both of them to do so, and to mean it, in the next few days, if not this evening." He turned back to Darcy. "You understand, I am sure, that sometimes it takes one some time to see the error of their ways."

Another stiff nod from Darcy, who, though he understood the truth of the statement, would rather have had their apologies now. "Yes, sir."

Just then, the butler announced that supper was served. Though the atmosphere was strained, Joseph and Grace, who had remained absolutely silent during the confrontation before the meal, kept up a lively conversation that included everyone present.

Chapter 14

Three days later, Elizabeth happily greeted Darcy once again. Her family was to attend another lecture, and he and Bingley had agreed to join them.

"Good evening, sir." She dipped a curtsey, the corners of her lips tilting upward in a happy smile. "Will you sit with me while we wait for my aunt and sister?" She gestured to the empty place beside her on the sofa.

Gardiner laughed. "Yes, do go sit beside her. She has been nearly unbearable in her excitement to see you."

Darcy blushed, but a grin lit up his face as he crossed the room and bowed in front of Elizabeth. "Thank you for saving me a seat." He looked back at his host. "And thank you, sir, for allowing me to join you."

Gardiner directed Bingley to an empty chair before he replied. "I was happy to oblige you, though if I had not, I have no doubt that the atmosphere in this home would have been rather chilly for a very long time." He chuckled.

Elizabeth rolled her eyes but laughed along with the gentlemen. She turned to Darcy. "How was your week?"

Darcy smiled at her, making her heart beat faster. "It passed rather quickly." He paused.

"I dined with my aunt and uncle a few days ago. They are here for the season."

Elizabeth's smile fell. She looked at her lap and clasped her hands together. "I see. How were they?"

"They were better before I arrived than after I left."

At Darcy's soft but firm words, Elizabeth looked up, her brow creasing.

"What do you mean?"

"I confronted my aunt and cousin about their words and actions toward you. My uncle was very unhappy to learn of it all."

Elizabeth nodded, her gaze moving away from Darcy for a moment as she remembered Judge Darcy's kindness to her. "He is very different from Mrs. Darcy and Mr. Andrew Darcy."

"Yes, he is, and I think he is just now realizing how different. He asked me to extend his apologies to you. My father had written to him, informing him that he approved of you and of me courting you. Uncle Joseph told my aunt about it, but it seems that she chose to ignore it. I do not know if Andrew ever knew." Darcy looked down for a moment before lifting his gaze back up to meet Elizabeth's. "He disparaged my father and I confess I touched him in anger. My uncle pulled me away or I would have done him some serious harm. I was nearly beyond reason."

Elizabeth stretched out her hand and touched his arm for a moment. "I am sorry he provoked you so. It is understandable to wish to defend a family member."

"Thank you."

Elizabeth and Darcy became lost in each other's eyes for a long moment, until Gardiner cleared his throat and loudly asked a question, which made them both jump and blush.

"Did your relatives give a reason for their interference?"

Darcy grimaced. "My aunt is the daughter of a tradesman ... her father was a solicitor in a town several miles from Pemberley. I noticed during my stay at Netherfield that her attitudes and behaviors towards those she considered inferior were often ungracious and unkind. My cousin Andrew has always been his mother's favorite, and it seems he has taken on her opinions as his own." Darcy paused and shook his head. He chuckled before he continued. "You should have seen their chagrin when they found out exactly who you are and what you do. I thought my aunt's head might burst open."

Elizabeth laughed, as did her uncle and Bingley.

The door opened, and Maddie poked her head in. "What is going on in here? I had to check the nursery to make sure my children were truly in bed and not in my drawing room." She pushed the wood panel in further and entered the parlor, followed by Jane.

Elizabeth and the gentlemen rose. Darcy, Bingley, and Gardiner bowed.

"We thought you were never going to be ready." Elizabeth's tease made everyone smile.

Maddie turned to Darcy. "Have you given thought to bringing your sister to dine with us next week?"

"I have." Darcy tipped his head. "She told me she would be delighted to meet your children and dine here in your home. I suspect she is lonely; she has no other children to play with here in town. At Pemberley, she can entertain herself with the servants' children or those of the tenants, but she knows no one in London who is not family, and they are all adults."

"I am glad she agreed! I will be sure to prepare Thomas and Margaret. They love to make new acquaintances. They will be happy to play with your sister."

"Then, it is settled." Gardiner clapped his hands together and rubbed them. "It is time for us to leave. We might even arrive a bit early."

With that, the six of them moved into the entry hall and donned their outerwear. They ascended into the coach and were soon on their way.

~~~***~~~
~~~

The following Tuesday, Darcy arrived for supper exactly on time. Elizabeth and Jane were waiting in the drawing room with Maddie and the two eldest children. Elizabeth was excited to see Darcy again, but she was also a bit nervous about meeting his sister. She wanted the girl to like her.

When they were announced, Darcy stepped into the room first, with Georgiana just behind him and holding his hand. Elizabeth could see from the younger girl's downcast eyes that she was shy, and her own nerves eased.

"Welcome!" Elizabeth's aunt greeted the guests. "Will you introduce me to your friend, Mr. Darcy?"

"Certainly." Darcy let go of his sister's hand and placed his on her back. "This is my sister, Miss Georgiana Darcy. Georgiana, this is Mrs. Gardiner, Miss Bennet, Miss Elizabeth, Master Thomas, and Miss Gardiner."

Georgiana curtseyed. Though her eyes never lifted much above her shoes, she softly greeted them. "I am pleased to make your acquaintance."

Elizabeth watched as Thomas bowed and Margaret gave a rather wobbly curtsey. She smiled at the three youngsters. "Well. That was rather momentous, would you not say?" She giggled, which caused all three children to look her way with varying degrees of alarm. "Miss Darcy, will you not join us on the settee?"

She watched as Georgiana looked to her brother and, when he nodded his permission, stepped slowly towards the children. Elizabeth made sure all three were seated safely, as the settee was rather high and their legs were rather short. Then, she sat in the midst of them and began asking questions. Within a few minutes, she had them conversing easily together, talking about lessons and dolls and games. She rose and left them to it, making her way to the sofa nearby, where Darcy sat waiting.

"You did that very well." Darcy watched his sister as he spoke. "She is very timid. I was worried she would not do well. It is heartening to see her bloom as she is."

Elizabeth shrugged. "I could see that right away. Sometimes all a person needs is to find a common activity or goal. My cousins were rather nervous, as well, but they are like my aunt, full of confidence. I knew they would get along well."

The evening passed quickly. The Gardiner children were allowed to take Georgiana upstairs and show her their nursery after supper, while the adults visited. When it was time to leave, Elizabeth laughed to herself at the way they clung to each other.

"Can Miss Darcy come back and play again?" Thomas asked his mother.

"You will have to ask Mr. Darcy about that, but I would happy to host her again, if he allows it."

Thomas looked at Darcy with wide eyes. He stuck his hand in his mouth for a moment, as though he were again a baby and not a breeched boy of six, but just when Elizabeth thought someone might have to prompt him, he pulled his hand away from his face, lifted his chin, and addressed the tall, dark-haired gentleman. "Can Miss Darcy come back and play again?"

"She can if she wishes to." He turned to his sister. "What do you say, Georgiana?"

"Oh, yes. I do wish to. May I please?"

"Since you and Master Gardiner and, I assume, Miss Gardiner?" Darcy paused and looked at Margaret with raised brows until she nodded and clapped. "Since you and Master Gardiner and Miss Gardiner have formed a friendship, and all of you have expressed an interest in continuing it, you may come back another day to play. I will consult with Mrs. Gardiner and Miss Fitzhugh and schedule a date."

Georgiana bounced on her toes. "Thank you, Brother."

Twin cries from the Gardiner children echoed her sentiment. "Thank you, Mr. Darcy!"

Soon, the Darcys were gone again and Elizabeth was left to daydream about the visit.

~~~***~~~
~~~

Over the course of the next fortnight, Darcy and Elizabeth, accompanied by Bingley, Jane, and the Gardiners, had several visits and outings. They toured museums, attended more lectures, and dined together. On one such outing, Elizabeth noted that Darcy seemed distracted and, perhaps, frustrated.

"Are you well, Mr. Darcy?" She looked up into his face as they wandered through the display of paintings.

Darcy jumped, as though surprised to be addressed. He sighed and turned his gaze from somewhere ahead of him to Elizabeth's curious face. "I am well. I apologize if I seem to be elsewhere."

"Has something happened?" She indicated her desire to stop and examine a large landscape.

Darcy tilted his head from side to side. Then, he sighed. "Do you remember me speaking to you of Lady Catherine de Bourgh?"

Elizabeth's brow creased. "She is one of your aunts, is she not?"

He nodded. "Yes, and she has long wished for me to marry her daughter, which I will not do." He turned her toward him. "She is not the one who holds my heart."

Elizabeth paused for a long moment, until the pounding in her chest at his declaration diminished enough that she could hear his words. "That is good to hear." She flashed him a grin.

Darcy chuckled, then turned serious again. "Lady Catherine and my cousin, Anne, arrived on my doorstep this morning, unannounced."

"Unannounced? That was rather …"

"Presumptuous of them, yes. It was, indeed." Darcy sighed. "I have a bad feeling about it. I do not understand why she is here. She refuses to listen when I tell her that my father told me he only wished for me to marry Anne if we were deeply in love. We are not and as I said, I do not intend to make my aunt happy about this. I sent a note to the earl. He can sometimes control her where others cannot." He shrugged. "I want her gone but cannot be so disrespectful as to kick her out without reason."

Elizabeth thought a moment. She indicated to her companion that she wished to walk on, and so they did. Finally, when she had worked out what to say, she spoke. "There is really nothing you can do. She is your elder, and not under your care. She is independent and can do as she wishes. Let us hope she is only there to express her displeasure and will soon go home." A thought struck her. "What brought her to town in the first place?"

Darcy shrugged. "As near as I can tell, she heard a rumor that I was escorting a young lady about town. Since that girl was not her daughter, she made it her business to discover who it was."

"Did you tell her?" Elizabeth tilted her head. "Come to think of it, someone must have written to her specifically to tell her. It is not as though we are attending balls and card parties together. No one who knows her should know me, at any rate."

Darcy was quiet for a long moment. "Theodosia. I wager it was my Aunt Darcy who wrote to Lady Catherine; she is the only person who knows about you. She has yet to apologize to either of us for her interference in our courtship."

Elizabeth bit her lip. "What is done is done, I suppose. What should we do now?"

Darcy lifted his shoulders again before dropping them. "Nothing. I am not giving you up. Lady Catherine can rant and rave all she wishes. It will not change anything. I will bear under it until she gives up and goes home. Let us hope it is sooner rather than later."

Elizabeth giggled. "Indeed."

Chapter 15

By the time Darcy returned home, his mother's sister and his cousin had gone to bed. Darcy was eager to do the same. His dreams of late had been filled with Elizabeth and what they would do when they married: the places they would visit, the people they would see, and the children they would raise. He looked forward to seeing where his dreams of her took him this night, so he rather impatiently went through his nightly routine and dismissed his valet as soon as he could. Soon, he was tucked up in his bed, smiling in his sleep.

The next morning, he awoke to the sun streaming over his face through a crack in the curtains. He stretched and yawned, then arose to begin his day.

"Smith, what is on my agenda for the evening?" His valet kept track of his social calendar as a part of his duties. The man needed to know what clothing his master was going to require from day to day.

"This evening, you are dining with the earl and countess."

"I had forgotten about that." Darcy thought for a moment while Smith prepared materials for shaving. "I suppose as long as it is formal, it does not matter what I wear. I should have asked them to invite Miss Bennet, but then, I am still in mourning and this is supposed to be a family party." He paused. "I am becoming impatient with all this propriety, if I am honest. I long to ask her to marry me now instead of waiting eight months to do it. We do not have to announce a betrothal to anyone but family members." He sighed and scrubbed his face with his hands. "I suppose, though, that the time will pass more quickly than I think it will."

"Very true." The valet turned to his employer, soaped-up shaving brush in hand.

Darcy leaned back in the chair and allowed Smith to scrape the beard off his face. He let his mind wander, and it eventually lighted upon his aunt and cousin. He waited for the servant to finish his work and wipe the soap off his face, then made his inquiry. "What have you heard belowstairs about Lady Catherine and Miss de Bourgh?"

"She has apparently been rather demanding. Lady Catherine has, I mean. She was so critical of the maid who opened up the guest room that the girl ran crying to the kitchen. It took the cook an hour to calm her down."

Darcy sighed. "I will tell Mrs. Bishop to give her a bonus in her pay. What else?"

"She was secretive about her conversations with her daughter. More so than usual, the footmen say. She stopped talking when they entered the room to serve the meal and did not open her lips again while they were there."

"Hm. I wonder what that was about." Darcy shook his head and rose to allow Smith to tie his cravat. "Keep your ears and eyes open. I do not know how long she intends to remain. I have an appointment with my attorney today, so that will keep me out of her reach for several hours, at least."

"Will you see Miss Elizabeth this afternoon?" Smith finished with the neck cloth and reached for Darcy's tailcoat.

"Sadly, no." Darcy sighed. "I wish I were. Her presence is a balm to my spirit."

Smith said nothing, but Darcy could have sworn the man rolled his eyes. He allowed the valet to assist him into the coat and then stood still as he fussed over it, brushing away invisible bits of lint and whatnot. Finally, Darcy had had enough, and he dismissed his servant and went out the door, successfully avoiding both Lady Catherine and Anne.

<div align="center">~~~***~~~</div>

Hours later, Darcy returned to the house.

"Good afternoon, Mr. Darcy. Welcome home." Mrs. Bishop accepted her employer's coat and hat and handed them to a footman to put away.

"Good afternoon." Darcy glanced up the stairs. "Has Lady Catherine made an appearance today?"

"No, sir. She has demanded meals for both her and Miss de Bourgh be delivered to their rooms and requested tea just about a quarter hour ago."

"Has she asked about me?"

"Yes, sir. Early this morning, she inquired as to your location. We told her you had an appointment but did not give out any details."

"Thank you." Darcy glanced up the stairs a second time. "Did she cause a disturbance?"

The housekeeper shrugged. "She raised her voice with Mr. Baxter, but he knows how to handle her. He reminded her that we are your employees and not hers, that our loyalty is to you, and that we do not give out information about your movements to anyone, no matter how closely they are related to you."

Darcy nodded. "Good." He paused. "There will be, once I am out of mourning, a second person to whom your loyalty will need to be extended."

"Sir?"

"I intend to ask a young lady for a formal courtship come October. Her name is Miss Elizabeth Bennet. I intend for her to become your mistress before another year has passed."

Mrs. Baxter smiled. "Elizabeth. What a lovely name. What is she like?"

A soft smile lifted Darcy's lips. "She is everything lovely. She is a happy, active sort of person, and very kind. And beautiful. Her eyes sparkle like diamonds." He sighed aloud. His attention was drawn to the housekeeper when she coughed.

"She sounds perfect. I wish you happy." Mrs. Bishop curtseyed. "I assume that you wish this information kept between us, given your current guests?"

"Yes, please do. The less my aunt knows, the better."

"Very good, sir."

Darcy dismissed his housekeeper and then strode down the hall to his study and ducked into it, locking the door behind him. He hoped to avoid Lady Catherine as much as possible until it was time to make the short drive to Matlock House.

~~~***~~~

That evening, Darcy waited at the bottom of the grand staircase for his aunt and cousin. Thankfully, the ladies did not take overly long to prepare, and soon they were descending the stairs together.

Darcy bowed. "Good evening, Aunt, Cousin."

"Darcy." Lady Catherine, a petite woman with iron gray hair, stood ramrod straight. "It is about time you made an appearance. I was beginning to think we would have no escort to my brother's home."
~~~

"I apologize for that. I had appointments to-day that could not be put off. However, I am here now. Shall we go?" He extended his arm toward the maids who waited with their outerwear behind them.

"Are you not going to speak to Anne? She is particularly lovely this evening, is she not?"

"My cousin is always impeccably turned out." Darcy greeted Anne. "I am happy you could join your mother for this visit. Do you intend to do any shopping or visiting?"

Anne clutched her hands together and bit her lip, glancing at her mother before replying. "I am uncertain what Mother has planned, beyond this evening."

"Our schedule is wholly dependent upon the actions of others." Lady Catherine's nose lifted. "We must remain flexible for now."

"I see." Darcy accepted his hat and greatcoat from the maid and slipped them on, waiting while his relatives did the same with theirs. Then, he escorted both of them out and into the waiting carriage. He was no more than seated on the rear-facing seat than his aunt began to berate him again about his supposed duty to her daughter.

"I cannot believe you would throw Anne over for someone of such low standing." Lady Catherine, as always, spoke imperiously. "It was the greatest wish of your mother for you to marry my daughter."

Darcy immediately put a stop to her words. "No, Aunt, it was not. If it was, she never said anything to me about it. All she told me was that, if I fell in love with Anne and she with me, I was free to marry her. Mother specifically said I was under no obligation to my cousin. I am not in love with your daughter and I have no intention of marrying her." He held up a hand when he heard Lady Catherine's intake of breath, though he knew she could not see him in the dark carriage. "This is neither the time nor the place for such a discussion. Not that there is anything to discuss. I will not marry my cousin. Anne, I am sorry if this hurts you, but I know you do not love me any more than I love you."

There was a long moment of silence before he heard his cousin's quiet reply.

"All is well. Do not trouble yourself."

The remaining minutes of the ride were enveloped in an awkward silence.

Finally, the trio was standing in the entry hall at Matlock House, greeting Lord and Lady Matlock, as well as Lord Tansley, Captain Fitzwilliam, and the two Fitzwilliam girls, Ladies Constance and Susan.

"It is good to see you, Darcy." Lady Matlock extended her hand to her nephew. "Are you well? We have hardly seen you since you arrived in town."

"I apologize, Aunt Audra. I have not felt much like visiting anyone, and have limited my visits." He glanced at Lady Catherine. "I have written to Uncle, keeping him abreast of my whereabouts and well-being."

Darcy saw his favorite aunt's eyes travel in the same direction his had before returning to him.

"He told me, but that is not the same as seeing you with my own eyes and being able to assure myself of your good health." She paused, flicking her glance again toward her sister-in-law and niece. When she spoke the next time, she lowered her voice so that only he could hear. "I am happy your lady is in town and you have reconnected with her. Your father wanted for you what he and Lady Anne had, and what your uncle and I have." She tilted her lips up in a small smile. "I know you will not allow anyone to persuade you against your heart. You are too much like your father for that, though not all of us in the family appear to understand it."

Darcy looked down, fighting to keep a smirk off his face. "Indeed." He looked up through his lashes at Lady Matlock and, seeing her wink, lowered his gaze once more, shaking his head and grinning.

The entire party retreated to the family parlor, which was located upstairs. Then, they chatted for a short while before supper was announced. They trooped back down in pairs to the dining room for the meal, Darcy offering his arm to his aunt, Lord Matlock giving his to his sister, Tansley escorting Anne, and Richard his sisters, one on each arm. They sat according to precedence, but their uneven number meant there was an empty space on Darcy's side of the table. He looked around and was relieved to see that Anne was seated to his uncle's left, on the same side of the table as he was, and that there was a space between Constance, who sat next to him, and Anne.

I will not have to deal with any reproachful looks or barbed questions, he thought. His cousin had refused to look at him and had barely touched his hand when he assisted her down from the carriage. Darcy turned his head to his meal and Lady Matlock.

When the courses were finished and his aunt had led the ladies back upstairs to the family parlor, Darcy, his cousins, and his uncle spent a short time sipping port and talking politics and current events. The conversation soon turned to other matters, with Lord Matlock making a request of his youngest son.

"Richard, when we go upstairs, I need you to go to my study and find that document. It will either be in the desk or in the safe in the library. Do you remember the combination?"

"I do." The captain gave a single nod. "What color is the ribbon?"

The earl shook his head. "I do not believe it is tied in that manner. I think it is simply a set of folded pages, three of them, sealed with wax and the imprint of Darcy's signet ring." He tilted his head and looked into the distance, his eyes darting back and forth as though trying to remember the details. "Yes, I think that is it." He looked at his nephew. "I have not opened it to see what your father said in this document. He entrusted it to me to hold for you until after the probate process had been completed."

Darcy lifted his shoulders and dropped them. "I cannot imagine what it might contain; the will was very specific."

"Has George Wickham come to you yet for his inheritance?" Richard lifted his brows along with his glass, taking a sip once he finished speaking.

"Not yet. I do not look forward to that conversation. However, my father and I spoke of it not long before he passed, and he laid out for me what his desires were, should Wickham be difficult about it."

"Good. Your father was thorough in everything he did." Lord Matlock lifted his glass. "To George Darcy."

His sons and nephew followed his lead. "To George Darcy."

They all took a sip and sat in silence for a long moment.

~~~***~~~

A quarter hour later, Darcy followed Richard into Lord Matlock's study, which was on the same floor as the family parlor but further
~~~

down the hall. Matlock and Tansley had joined the ladies while Richard and Darcy looked for the document.

The Matlock's house in town was much like Darcy's, in that it was larger than most of the surrounding homes. The second story of the house held a library, the earl's study, a water closet, and a smallish room the mistress liked to call her sewing room on one side, and the family parlor and master's and mistress' chambers on the other side, with their own shared sitting room. The study was the next-to-the last door on the left, and that is the one Darcy and Richard went into. There was a door to the library on the wall to their right.

"You look in the desk," Richard said as they entered, waving his hand toward the large piece of furniture on their left. "I will check the safe in the book room."

With a silent nod, Darcy walked behind the massive wooden desk and began pulling open drawers and searching them, beginning with the shallow one in the center. He had just opened the top drawer on the left when he heard the lock on the room's door snick. He looked up, startled, to find Anne with her back leaning against the wooden panel. She was without her eyewear. His brow creased as he took in more of her appearance.

"Are you well, Anne? What happened to your spectacles? Did you lose them?" He paused as she moved closer and the light of the candelabra highlighted her gown, which was missing its fichu. Her capped sleeves had been pulled down, exposing her shoulders and making her gown seem as though it might fall off her less-than-full-bosomed body. "Can I help you find them?" He went still, a frisson of unease snaking up his spine.

Anne sashayed closer toward him. He noticed a movement behind her and saw Richard just beyond the doorway to the library, watching with apparent interest what was happening. Darcy pulled his attention back to his female cousin, who appeared not to notice the captain. He suspected the reason for that to be that her eyesight was known to be so poor without the spectacles that she could not find her way out of a sack. When she finally spoke, she pulled him away from his contemplations.

"You can help me by fulfilling your duty toward me." She stopped no more than two paces in front of him.

"As I said in the carriage, I was never engaged to you. My father was explicit about that. The entire idea of a betrothal between us was a creation of your mother. Mine never endorsed it. No contracts were signed. I am not honor-bound to you."

Anne had taken one more step towards him but stopped, her countenance reddening. "You are! I have been told for as long as I remember that we were destined for each other.

I have had no season, no presentation, because I was engaged to you."

Darcy shook his head. "I am not, and I refuse to argue with you about it. I do not know what you are about, following me in here like you have, but this is not the way to convince me of anything."

Anne took a deep breath and another half-step toward him. "Please." Darcy could hear the urgency in her voice. "I am desperate to get away from my mother. You do not know what it is like. I have to get out from under her thumb." She shook her head and whispered, "Do not make me do this."

Darcy shrugged. "I am sorry you are unhappy, but I am not the answer." He was unprepared for what happened next.

Anne threw herself at him, grabbing his lapels and clutching them. She pressed herself to him. "You *are* the answer!"

Darcy immediately began to back away from her. He took hold of her wrists and held them while he backed up. Then, he let go. To his horror, Anne reached up and took hold of the neckline of her gown and pulled. The sound of ripping cloth filled the room as she exposed herself to him.

"Now you have to marry me. I have compromised you. Or, I should say and will say to others, you have compromised me."

Darcy's eyes had widened at his cousin's actions. She was now completely exposed to his eyes. She had worn no corset and had torn both gown and chemise. Her almost-nonexistent bosom was framed by the remains of her clothing. Horror filled him and he turned away.

"No, he does not."

Richard's deep, angry voice came from directly behind Darcy, and he turned to see that Anne had moved to face the captain. From the movements of her arms, Darcy suspected she was frantically trying to cover herself with what was left of her bodice.

"Darcy will never marry you because I will not allow it." Richard's eyes narrowed on Anne. He stood stiffly, his posture and mien giving clear indication of his anger. "Why should he give up the love of his life to save your miserable, scheming hide?" His eyes raked her up and down. "Once our parents learn of this, it will be me you marry. And they *will* learn of it. However ..." He examined her form again and a smirk twisted his lips. "I will do as you were going to do to Darcy and tell them that I am the one who ripped your clothing, just to make sure it happens."

"Richard ..." Darcy was becoming uneasy at the other man's words. He was clearly enraged.

The captain held up a hand. "No, Cousin. Let me handle this as I see fit. This apple has clearly not fallen far from the tree." He glanced from Anne, who until now he had not taken his eyes off of, to Darcy. "You need to ask Father how it was that his sister came to marry Lewis de Bourgh." His eyes moved back to Anne and his jaw clenched, a muscle in his cheek twitching. "No, this apple did not fall far at all."

"My mother will not make me marry you." Anne had apparently gathered her courage and straightened her spine. "You are nothing but a penniless soldier."

Richard laughed. "You think that if it makes you feel better."

Darcy knew what Anne seemed not to. Their cousin had been the beneficiary of a small fortune from his mother's bachelor brother. Additionally, he had saved and invested part of his allowance every quarter. Captain Richard Fitzwilliam did not need to remain a soldier. He chose to as a way to keep himself busy, and because he felt a great deal of patriotism toward his homeland.

"You cannot marry in anger, Cousin." Darcy pleaded with the captain, hoping to make him see reason. "What sort of life would that be for either of you?"

"Oh, I assure you I will not always be angry with her." Richard pulled his tail coat off and tossed it over Anne's shoulders. He reached for her elbow, grasping it and turning her toward the door. "I have been thinking about marrying for many months. I tire of soldiering and have seen things no man should. Our cousin is pretty and available. She wants to marry, she comes with a sizeable dowry, and she has a desire to be away from her mother. You know how much of a trial I find Lady Catherine. Anne will get what she wants, and I will get what I want. All but our aunt will obtain their desires." He paused in his progress toward the door, stopping himself and Anne to look back at Darcy. "Who knows what sort of rake she might try this with next. Better I marry her and save the family name than she follow in her mother's footsteps any further." He began to move again, urging Anne to walk into the hall.

Darcy followed, his brow creased.

A roar arose when the trio walked into the parlor.

"What is this?" Lady Matlock rose, her hand over her heart.

"What have you done to my daughter?" Lady Catherine surged to her feet, her words angry but her expression of them less so. Darcy noticed a gleam in her eye.

"Hush." Lord Matlock had risen, also, and now insisted on quiet from the ladies. "Son, what is going on?"

Richard did exactly as he had told Anne he would, insisting he had compromised her so he could marry her. Darcy watched Lady Catherine as his cousin told the tale. Her eyes darted between her nephews and daughter and he knew she had been aware of the plan. Further, he suspected she was angry at the way it had played out. She wanted Darcy and always had, not another Fitzwilliam. Only Darcys had Pemberley.

Chapter 16

The next day, Elizabeth listened in fascinated horror as Darcy explained to her and her family what had happened after dinner at Matlock House. She and Jane both sat with their hands over their mouths as he described the consternation of the earl and countess when their youngest son had declared he was going to marry Anne de Bourgh.

Maddie, who was apparently not as shocked at what she heard as Elizabeth was, shook her head before she asked Darcy a question. "I suspect there is more to what Miss de Bourgh did than you have described?"

Red instantly rushed up from Darcy's collar to his hairline. "Yes, there is. I have not described everything."

Elizabeth's brows rose as she dropped her hand to her lap? "What do you mean?" She watched as her beloved's color deepened and he stammered.

"I think what he means is that his cousin completely exposed herself." Maddie looked from Elizabeth to Darcy. "Is that not so?"

Darcy nodded slowly. "It is, unfortunately." He shifted in his seat.

Elizabeth felt all the anguish of their past separation rise up inside her again. Swallowed down bile as she realized exactly what had happened. She could see that Darcy was uncomfortable. "While I am admittedly curious to learn more, I suspect I should be happy for now with what you have said." She paused, looking at her aunt, sister, and uncle, all of whom were nodding their agreement. She looked back at Darcy. "What will happen now? Will your cousins marry? What does this mean for us?"

"They will marry. Once my uncle heard the particulars, he insisted upon it. He sent Richard home with me at the end of the night and forced the de Bourgh ladies to spend the night at his home." He shrugged. "I suppose he wished to give them no more opportunity to come at me."

Gardiner had listened to the entire tale in silence until this point. Now, he gestured to his guest, urging him to say more. "Did the earl share the tale of his sister?"

Elizabeth's gaze darted from her uncle to Darcy. She watched him nod.

"He did. It seems Lady Catherine was desperate to marry. She was in her fifth season and had received no offers. With her dowry, which the old earl had supplemented as added inducement to potential suitors, she should have had gentlemen beating down the door. However, her caustic tongue kept them away in droves. When she entered her final season, she had already spent two of her four years throwing herself in the paths of various gentlemen, without success. She noticed Sir Lewis de Bourgh at the beginning of her fifth season. He was a baronet and practically engaged to the daughter of a duke. She decided he would do, despite not being of the peerage." Darcy paused when a maid entered the room with a tray of tea things. After she had curtseyed and made her exit, he continued his tale.

"Lady Catherine stalked him like he was a prize deer, presenting herself before him and spreading tales about him to make him look bad to his love interest. She tried to befriend the lady, even." Darcy shook his head. "As that season came to a close, she became desperate. She attended a ball in her parents' home, having snipped the seams of her gown when she was dressing and leaving off certain … important articles of clothing."

Elizabeth saw him blush anew at his last words, all the while experiencing an ever-increasing feeling of revulsion for the way his aunt had conducted herself.

"She followed him into an empty room, which he had retreated to in order to use a chamber pot, and threw herself at him. Uncle could not say for certain exactly what happened, but another guest entered the room to find my aunt, completely exposed to her waist, and Sir Lewis with his pants around his knees." Darcy shrugged. "The old earl was embarrassed at his daughter's actions and desperate at get rid of her. He pressured Sir

Lewis, then threatened to ruin him. In the end, Sir Lewis agreed and they were married. My aunt was triumphant, but Sir Lewis was the opposite. He spent the entire period before their wedding in a state of drunkenness, and a good deal of his marriage after that.

"She did give him two sons, but they died in a carriage accident, along with her husband. Anne was injured in the same accident."

"So, she ended up with his name and estate." Gardiner shook his head. "It never pays to underestimate a desperate person."

Darcy nodded his agreement. "Indeed." He shuddered. "I can guarantee you, I never will. I am happy Richard was there, though not even a compromise would make me marry Anne. She would have been left ruined."

Elizabeth smiled softly at him. "I am also happy for the captain's presence." She paused and looked out the window. "The weather is not terrible today. Would you like to walk with me?" She turned to Jane. "Would you like to come along?"

Jane blushed. "Mr. Bingley is to call this afternoon. I would rather wait here for him."

"I had forgotten!" Elizabeth turned to Darcy. "I am surprised he did not come with you."

"I did not think to ask him along, but I was aware that he was calling here quite a bit on his own." Darcy lifted a shoulder. "I would love to walk with you; we can go now with a maid or wait for my friend to arrive."

Elizabeth bit her lip and looked at Jane.

"Do not feel obligated to wait if you would rather go now, Sister. I do not feel much like walking today, anyway." Jane smiled serenely.

"Very well." Elizabeth turned to her aunt. "May we take Sally with us? She is an excellent walker and can easily keep up."

Maddie smirked. "You may. I will call for her while you gather your things." She rose to do as she had said she would.

Elizabeth looked at Darcy, who stood and offered her his hand. She took it and came to her feet, following him into the entry hall. A few minutes later, they were walking out the door, the maid following.

The strolled up the street in silence, Elizabeth's small hand tucked into the crook of Darcy's elbow, snugged up tightly to his side. They walked two or three streets down, then crossed to a small grassy lot between two businesses that served the neighborhood as a park of sorts.

"Miss Elizabeth, I have a question for you."

Her head turned from its contemplation of the world around her to look up at Darcy's face. "Ask away. I am certain I have a reply of some sort." She grinned when he chuckled and lifted her fingers to kiss them.

"I am still in mourning, but have for days now been cursing the traditions that prevent me from declaring myself to you." He paused, squinting up into the sun for a moment. "The incident with my cousin last night was a stark reminder that anything can happen at any time to alter the course of our lives. In the blink of an eye, we could have been separated forever. I could not bear it if that happened, and I am no longer willing to risk my happiness." He stopped and turned toward her, forcing Elizabeth to stop, as well.

"Will you marry me, with the intention that our ceremony will be held immediately after my mourning is over at the end of September? We will have to keep it quiet; I will tell my Matlock relations and my sister, and you will tell your London relations and your parents, but the world at large will remain in the dark to avoid gossip. Will you make me the happiest of men?"

Elizabeth looked down as she considered his words. She felt his hands, which he had used to grasp hers, tighten and looked up to see him bite his lip.

"I guess we have been quietly courting all this time, have we not?" she asked. She watched as his countenance lightened.

"I suppose we have. What are you saying?"

"I never again wish to experience the fear I just did as you recounted your story. Nor do I want to feel the terror of a potentially permanent separation. As you said, lives can be altered in the blink of an eye." She paused.

"Yes, I will marry you. I love you too much to risk losing you."

"Thank you, my love." Darcy's shoulders sagged. He kissed her hand. "You and your mother can plan the wedding while we wait. We could marry the day after my mourning ends, on September 30th."

Elizabeth's brows drew together. "Can the banns be called while you are still wearing black?"

Darcy shook his head. "I do not know, but I plan to purchase a license. I can do that ahead of time and have everything ready to go. Then, all I must do is work with your father on your settlement." Excitement colored his voice. He glanced around. Then, seeing no onlookers, he took a smiling Elizabeth in his arms. "Thank you. You have made me the happiest of men. I love you."

Elizabeth grinned and, seeing his head lower, lifted her face to accept his kiss. They quickly became lost in each other, until a sound made them jump apart.

Darcy turned toward the Gardiner home, holding his arm out for Elizabeth to take. "Shall we inform your family of our decision?"

"Yes, we should." Elizabeth happily took his arm and walked at his side down Gracechurch Street. She looked up at this tall gentleman who held the key to her heart and sighed happily. She was looking forward to her marriage, because she knew it was better than she would ever be able to imagine.

Chapter 17

17 March, 1806

Longbourn

Darcy guided his horse toward the front steps of the Bennet residence. He had not seen Elizabeth in well over a fortnight, and he was eager to hear her voice and look deep into her fine eyes.

Pulling the animal to a halt, he glanced up at the door while throwing his right leg over the gelding's rump and lowering it to the ground. He looked down to pull his left foot out of the stirrup and remove something from his saddlebag, tucking it into his pocket, then handed the reins to a waiting groom. He tossed the boy a coin before brushing off his clothes and adjusting his hat. His attention was caught by the sound of the front door opening. He looked up to see his betrothed come charging outside.

"Fitzwilliam!"

Darcy took two steps forward, to the bottom of the shallow set of stairs that led to the porch, a delighted grin causing creases to form around his eyes. He opened his arms to catch Elizabeth, who had launched herself at him from the top stair. He pulled her close, burying his nose in her hair. "Did you miss me, my love?"

"I did! It has been ever so long since I have seen you!" Elizabeth pulled back, removing her arms from around his neck to frame his face with her hands. "Are you well?"

"I am, especially now that I have you in my arms once more."

"Lizzy, why do you not invite the gentleman inside?"

Darcy looked up to see Mr. Bennet standing in front of the door, one brow raised above his spectacles and a stern expression upon his face. Immediately, Elizabeth let go of his face and spun around.

"I was getting to that." Her hands landed on her hips. "I am marrying the man in six months and have been separated from him – for a second time, may I remind you – for weeks. A hug is required in this instance."

Bennet blinked, seemingly taken aback at Elizabeth's words. He took a step backwards, then spoke. "Very well, then." He paused. "I should reprimand you for your insolence, but since I am the one who taught you to speak your mind, I suppose I would look stupid if I did. Therefore, I will take the dose of my own medicine and let that go. However, you have had your hug and now should bring Mr. Darcy inside. Your mother is very excited, and I can only hold her back so long."

Darcy stood speechless at this interaction. His eyes darted from father to daughter. He was relieved to see her arms lower.

"Very well, then." Elizabeth lifted her chin. "I apologize if I was too forward just now."

Bennet lifted a hand as he began to turn toward the door. "No, no, none of that. All is well. Just come on inside the house, both of you."

Shaking his head, Darcy turned back to his betrothed. "It is my fault this happened. I should have let you go sooner."

Elizabeth shook her head. "No, it is not your doing. Papa has been teasing me beyond bearing for two days. It serves him right that I spoke sharply to him. Besides, he did teach me to be this way. He cannot now demand blind obedience." She sniffed. "If I want to embrace the man I am engaged to, I will do so. Who is going to gossip about that?"

Darcy cleared his throat. He had never before seen Elizabeth when she was vexed in such a way. "Indeed." He paused and tried to keep a sober expression. "Is this what I have to look forward to after we marry?" His lips twitched, despite his best effort to prevent it.

Elizabeth peered up at him, her eyes narrowed. She was quiet for a long moment. It was only when he winked that she rolled her eyes and tucked her arm under his. "As a matter of fact, yes. You may as well get used to it now." She giggled then, and squeezed his arm to her chest.

Darcy chuckled. "Shall we make your parents happy and repair to the drawing room?" When she consented, he escorted her into the house.

"Welcome back to Longbourn, Mr. Darcy!" Mrs. Bennet curtseyed. "You will stay to dine with us, will you not?"

Darcy bowed to his future mother-in-law. "I will; I thank you for the invitation."

"Excellent!" The matron settled herself on the sofa. "Today's dinner is a special one, for it is Lizzy's birthday celebration. The cook has prepared all her favorite dishes."

Darcy looked from Mrs. Bennet to Elizabeth. "I am happy I was able to make it here in time for such a momentous occasion." He lifted one corner of his lips. "I have a present for you."

Elizabeth lifted a brow. "You mean, something more than your presence?"

Darcy chuckled. "I do. Surely you did not think, once you informed me of its date, that I would allow the anniversary of your birth to pass without acknowledgement?"

Elizabeth blushed and shrugged. "I did not know. However, I am happy to hear that you did not, for I love presents nearly as much as I love to laugh."

"Do you want to open it now, or would you rather wait?"

She lifted her shoulders. "I do not have a preference, to be honest."

Darcy smirked. "Then I will follow mine, which is that you attend to it immediately, for I wish to see your reaction and do not care to wait for it."

Elizabeth laughed. "Very well, then." She held her hand out, palm up. "Give it to me."

Darcy pulled the package out of his pocket and laid it in her hand. He watched intently as she examined the plain brown paper.

Elizabeth glanced up at him, then pulled at the string that tied it all up. Inside was a letter and another package, this one wrapped in pretty paper and tied with a lavender ribbon.

"Read the note first." Darcy watched her as she followed his suggestion, placing the package on her lap and breaking the seal on the missive. He kept his eyes glued to her as her hand lifted to cover her mouth and her eyes filled with tears.

"What does it say?" Mrs. Bennet's voice intruded into the moment.

"Yes, what does it say? You cannot keep it to yourself when we have all witnessed the giving of the gift." If Darcy remembered correctly, the speaker of those words was the youngest Bennet, Miss Lydia.

"Oh." Elizabeth looked startled. She glanced at Darcy. "I do not know ..."

Lydia squealed. "Is it a love letter, then? Does it say things we should not hear?" She rushed toward her elder sister, hand out.

Elizabeth moved the missive out of the younger girl's reach. "No, it is not inappropriate. However, it *is* a love letter and none of your concern." She nodded decidedly and folded the note, tucking it under her leg. Then, she picked up the package and admired the ribbon for a few minutes. Finally, she pulled on the end and it fell away. She unwrapped the box, carefully folding the colored paper and placing it with the letter. Then, she lifted the lid of the box.

Darcy watched Elizabeth's reaction carefully. His gift was a choker that had been his mother's. The stones went well with his betrothed's coloring and he hoped she liked them.

"How beautiful!" Elizabeth slowly lifted the necklace out of the box and turned to him. "I am honored that you would give me such a lovely item, and one that I suspect holds much sentimental value to you. Thank you, my love. Will you help me put it on?"

Darcy breathed a sigh of relief that she liked it so much. He took it from her and, when she had turned around, hung it around her neck and closed the clasp. "It is not every day a lady turns six and ten," he said. "Such an occasion requires jewels." He smiled into her eyes as she turned to face him once more.

After sitting through the effusions of the Bennet ladies over his gift, he asked Elizabeth if she wished to walk in the garden with him. She readily agreed, and her mother set Mary as their chaperone. Within a few minutes, they were wandering the paths, arm in arm.

Elizabeth laughed as she looked toward the bench that her sister had taken over, book in hand. "Mary is such an obliging chaperone, is she not?"

Darcy glanced across and noted the younger girl's position. "She is. I am thankful for it." He laid his free hand over hers, which was curled around his forearm. He laced their fingers together and sighed happily.

"Will you tell me what happened with Mr. Wickham?"

Darcy nodded and gathered his thoughts. "He was on his way to visit one of the tenants who had come to him with a problem. He took one of the newly broken horses. He told the stable master that he wished to give the animal some additional experience with a rider, as that particular mare had been difficult to train." He shook his head. "Apparently, she threw him off. We found a snake, crushed to death, nearby. My guess is, she became startled and bucked, and Wickham was unable to hold on. His neck was broken; he must have landed on it. My one comfort is that his death was mercifully quick."

"I am so sorry." Elizabeth squeezed his arm and leaned her head against his shoulder for a long moment. When she lifted it, she asked another question. "Your letter said Mr. George Wickham approached you?"

Darcy snorted. "Yes. All these months after his godfather passed away, he finally came to discover what his inheritance was."

"Was it a terrible experience?"

Darcy shrugged, looking moodily off into the distance. Then, he sighed. "He is just such a waste ... of a good education, of an intelligent mind, and, frankly, of an excellent patronage." He paused and took a deep breath. "George came to me, apparently expecting more out of my father's will than he got. He outright stated his belief that my father left him more than the thousand pounds he did. Then, he refused the living. I had expected him to do that, and offered him money in exchange, as Papa had told me to before he died."

"Dare I ask how much?"

"He wanted ten thousand pounds. He walked away with three thousand."

Elizabeth gasped. "So much! He cannot now come back on you for presentation of the living, can he?"

Darcy shook his head. "No, he cannot. I had him sign both a receipt for the funds and a written promise that he would never make a claim for the living in the future."

"Good. I hope we never see him again, then."

Darcy glanced at his companion as she spoke, and smiled at her determined look.

"I cannot agree more, my love." Darcy squeezed her fingers. "I have not heard from Bingley lately. How does his courtship with your sister go?"

Elizabeth grinned. "He visits Gracechurch Street every single day. My aunt says he is there at one every afternoon, like clockwork."

Darcy laughed. "Bingley sometimes seems a little scattered, but promptness is one of his better qualities. I suspect his father instilled that in him."

"It is an excellent trait in a tradesman, according to my uncle. Would that more gentlemen learned to be that way. I am happy Mr. Bingley did." She peeked up at him. "You are prompt, as well, and I appreciate that."

Darcy smiled again. "I would not leave you waiting for the world, not willingly. It smacks too much of our separation last year."

Elizabeth nodded. "Which is why I appreciate it so." She looked toward the path that led to Netherfield. "Your family has not yet moved away?"

Darcy shook his head. "No, Uncle Joseph extended the lease until Michaelmas. He wanted me to be able to court you here." He sighed. "He forced Andrew to apologize to me.

You should expect one when he visits after his term at school."

Elizabeth nodded. "Did he mean it?"

Darcy shrugged. "That I do not know, but he said the words prettily enough and that will have to do. He has lost my trust, as has my aunt, who has yet to apologize." He looked down at his beloved. "Has she done so to you?"

She shook her head. "No, she has not. She has barely been cordial. Frosty, is how Mary put it when they met at last month's assembly."

"Well, Uncle will straighten it out when he arrives in June. I suspect, though, that they will give the lease up after that, and not extend it again."

He felt his betrothed's shrug against his arm. "It will be no great loss to the neighborhood the way things stand." She paused. "We do not marry until the second of October. If they vacate before Michaelmas, where will you stay?"

"Probably at the inn in Meryton. It is close enough, and while it will not be the same as staying in a private home, it will only be for two or three days. I can bear it. Georgiana will stay with the Matlocks until after our wedding trip; they will bring her here. I need to remember to ask your mother if she has room to accommodate them here at Longbourn. Otherwise, I must make reservations for them, as well."

Elizabeth nodded. "I am certain she will make room for an earl and countess." She laughed, then fell silent and laid her head on his shoulder once more as they began their third circuit around the gardens. "Speaking of bearing things, how are Lady Catherine and your cousin dealing with that wedding?"

Darcy's brows shot up. "Did I not tell you?"

Elizabeth lifted her head and looked at him. "Tell me what?"

"Uncle Henry went to the bishop and purchased a special license. Anne and Richard were married the day I was called back to Pemberley. Neither Lady Catherine nor her daughter wished me to be in attendance, so I did not discover it until the earl wrote me about it. Richard wanted the special license specifically so I could be there. He intended a private ceremony at Matlock House with no guests other than family." Darcy shrugged. "He was outnumbered, however, and the earl and countess were not willing to fight Lady Catherine about it."

"I am sorry. Were you terribly disappointed?"

"No, not really. It would have been nice to be there for the captain and to see with my own eyes that Anne was safely married, and not to me, but it was not that important. I gave Richard a very nice wedding gift before I left." Darcy shrugged. "Lady Catherine will eventually have to forgive me, as will Anne."

"Is the captain still angry with her?"

"Oh, no. He got over it quickly, as he said he would. He is a practical sort and the marriage helps both him and her. Anne did not expect love; she did not have those sorts of feelings for me, either. She just wanted to be married and away from her mother." He chuckled. "I expect that is Lady Catherine's reason for being angry about the whole thing. Richard will have no compunction about holding her at arm's length, where she knew I would let her have her way simply to keep the peace. She is furious that she cannot control him."

Elizabeth laughed. "I almost feel sorry for her."

Darcy was surprised. "You do?"

She nodded. "Almost. She has been in control of everything around her for a very long time; most of her life, if I understand what you have said correctly. Now, she will have no one's life to run but her own."

Darcy laughed. "I see your point." He sighed happily. "I love doing this with you, walking paths amongst beautiful flowers and bushes, holding you close." He stopped, turning them so they faced each other. "I love you, and I have missed you more than I can say. I want to do just this every night for the rest of our lives. What do you say?"

Elizabeth smiled as she lifted a hand to cup his cheek. "I say I want the same. I love you, as well."

Darcy drew her close, glancing over his shoulder to make sure Mary's nose was still in her book. Then, he leaned down and pressed his lips to his beloved's, feeling again the tingle that shot from his mouth to his heart.

~~~***~~~

On the second day of October in the year 1806, Elizabeth made Darcy the happiest of men. He cherished the knowledge that he alone held the key to her heart, and he vowed to himself to keep it safe forever.

~~~

About the Author

Zoe Burton first fell in love with Jane Austen's books in 2010, after seeing the 2005 version of Pride and Prejudice on television. While making her purchases of Miss Austen's novels, she discovered Jane Austen Fan Fiction; soon after that she found websites full of JAFF. Her life has never been the same. She began writing her own stories when she ran out of new ones to read.

Zoe lives in a 100-plus-year-old house in the snow-belt of Ohio with her Boxer, Jasper. She is a former Special Education Teacher, and has a passion for romance in general, *Pride and Prejudice* in particular, and stock car racing.

Connect with Zoe Burton

Email:

zoe@zoeburton.com

Facebook:

https://www.facebook.com/ZoeBurtonBooks

https://www.facebook.com/groups/BurtonsBabes/

Pinterest:

https://www.pinterest.com/zoeburtonauthor/

Instagram:

https://www.instagram.com/zoeburtonauthor/

Website:

https://zoeburton.com

Join my mailing list:

https://mailchi.mp/ee42ccbc6409/zoeburtonsignup

Support me at Patreon:

https://www.patreon.com/zoeburtonauthor

Me at Austen Authors:

http://austenauthors.net/zoe-burton/

More by Zoe Burton

Regency Single Titles:

I Promise To…

Lilacs & Lavender

Promises Kept

Bits of Ribbon and Lace

Decisions and Consequences

Mr. Darcy's Love

Darcy's Deal

The Essence of Love

Matches Made at Netherfield

Darcy's Perfect Present

Darcy's Surprise Betrothal

To Save Elizabeth

Darcy Overhears

Merry Christmas, Mr. Darcy!

Darcy's Secret Marriage

Darcy's Christmas Compromise

Darcy's Predicament

Darcy's Uneasy Betrothal

Darcy's Yuletide Wedding

Darcy's Unwanted Bride

Darcy's Favorite

Darcy's Christmas Scheme

Victorian Romance:

A MUCH Later Meeting

WESTERN ROMANCE:

Darcy's Bodie Mine

Bundles:

Darcy's Adventures

Forced to Wed

Promises

Mr. Darcy Finds Love (available exclusively to newsletter subscribers)

The Darcy Marriage Series Books 1-3

Mr. Darcy, My Hero

Coming Together

Christmas in Meryton

The Darcy Marriage Series:
Darcy's Wife Search

Lady Catherine Impedes

Caroline's Censure

Pride & Prejudice & Racecars

Darcy's Race to Love

Georgie's Redemption

Darcy's Caution

www.ingramcontent.com/pod-product-compliance
Lightning Source LLC
Chambersburg PA
CBHW071257190726
48292CB00007B/2574